Flight 39
Phillip P. Peterson

Translated by

Jenny Piening

Edited by

Laura Radosh

Flight 39

1

Georg jumped off the tram at the first stop on Rosenheimer Straße. He was the only passenger to alight. It was a cold, wet November evening, and most people were probably home warming themselves in front of a fire. It had already been dark when he had arrived at Munich Central Station from Ulm.

He waited until the tram had rumbled into motion again, its bell ringing, before setting off down Rosenheimer Straße. A car came slowly down the street toward him and he could make out two men wearing peaked caps and black uniforms sitting inside. Probably SS. Georg quickened his pace and looked down at the ground, like a worker who simply wanted to get home as quickly as possible in this nasty weather.

The men in the car passed him without a second glance. When he ventured a look over his shoulder, he saw it turning onto Hochstraße. Georg continued slowly on his way, ignoring the right turn onto Schleibinger Straße, and reached his destination a few minutes later. He was standing in front of the large stone archway that led into the grounds of the Bürgerbräukeller. He lingered for a moment in front of the archway, and scanned the area around the beer hall. He was sure he didn't look suspicious, but he wanted to be on the safe side. He couldn't see any soldiers or SS men. The only person to come stumbling through the gate was a drunkard in a ragged, dirty suit, but he didn't even give Georg a second glance.

Georg took a deep breath and walked purposefully

through the stone archway toward the main entrance of the beer hall. The sound of laughter and piano music floated through the window into the courtyard.

What was that? He noticed a movement from the corner of his eye and swung round. Georg wasn't paranoid, but sometimes he thought he was being watched: people who looked at him a second too long, like Gestapo collaborators given the task of watching him; cars that he thought he had seen minutes before, as if they had driven in a circle in order not to lose sight of him; uniformed SS soldiers scanning a crowd as if searching for him. But Georg knew he was imagining it, because if somebody had really found out what he was planning, he would have been arrested long ago.

With a firm tug, Georg pulled open the entrance door, walked through the anteroom, and noticed to his relief that nobody was loitering in the corridor. The few guests who were here today must all be in the bar. He walked past the cloakroom and pulled open the door to the main hall. It was—as always—unlocked. He closed the door behind him. Enough light came through the windows to dimly illuminate the vaulted room. The hall was large enough to hold thousands of people, and there was room up in the gallery for hundreds more. He walked swiftly to the nearest staircase that led up to the gallery. After the many nights he had spent here carrying out his plan, he could have found his way blindfolded. Once at the top, he crept past a row of tables, bent double, until he had reached the central pillar, which reached down to the speaker's podium. Glancing around to double-check that nobody was looking, he pressed his right ear to the wooden cladding of the pillar.

Georg held his breath and listened to the regular ticking of the twin-clock mechanism inside.

Then he knelt down, took a small pocketknife out of his jacket and pried open the wood paneling. Beneath it was a suitcase-sized cavity in the brickwork of the pillar, which he had painstakingly hewn out at night over the past few weeks. Several days ago he had deposited the explosives, which he had stolen while working at a quarry in Königsbronn earlier in the year. He inserted the detonator in the pillar. Georg had come up with a construction whereby three nails were driven into the firing caps of three blasting cartridges. He was especially proud of the clock mechanism. The clock mechanism …

Georg was a skilled craftsman, but the construction of his bomb had been extremely complex and he had worked on it for weeks in his workshop in Munich. He wanted to be absolutely sure his plan would work, and that's why he hadn't inserted just *one* clock, but two, so that the fuse would be triggered, even if one of the clocks stopped. He had also wanted to set the mechanism several days in advance, which had required a special construction. Today he was only there to make sure that everything was working. To his satisfaction he saw that both clock mechanisms were accurate to the minute, even though he had set them two days ago. They were precision mechanisms, he had made sure of that.

He checked the clocks again. The event was due to start at eight thirty and last several hours, twenty past nine seemed like a good time for the bomb to go off. Georg considered feverishly whether there was anything he could have forgotten. But he had been absolutely meticulous in his planning and now he would have to let it take its course.

He closed the clock case and attached the cork lid. Finally, he replaced the wood cladding on the pillar and assured himself that nothing indicated that it had been tampered with.

Installing the bomb had been straightforward, despite the many hours it had taken him. A few days ago, a member of staff had spotted him up in the gallery as he had been waiting for the Bürgerbräukeller to close, but he'd managed to talk his way out of it with some far-fetched story about needing to squeeze a boil. The next day he had simply tried again and had been able to continue with his work uninterrupted. The hall was opened in the morning and locked up again at night. As the Bürgerbräukeller had two entrances on different streets, a few locals used it as a shortcut to get from Kellerstraße to Löwenstraße, so that passersby were nothing unusual here. Even now, one day before the Führer's talk, there were no security measures in place whatsoever. Georg brushed a few bits of loose plaster from the pillar.

It was now after midnight and the bar would already be closed. Georg walked round the gallery to a little storeroom; its entrance was covered only by a folding screen. During his nights here, he had created a little hiding place for himself out of a few boxes and now he curled up behind them. He tried to get some sleep, which was difficult. Restlessly, he tossed and turned on the cold floor and mulled over what he might have forgotten. Finally, at around three in the morning, he fell into a fitful sleep.

He was awoken suddenly by a noise: the turning of a key in a lock. It came from the front of the building, where the kitchen was located. Georg looked at his pocket watch. It was already six in the morning, but still dark of course. The first employees from the kitchen had obviously arrived for the day.

He got up, and rearranged the boxes so that nobody would notice they had been moved. Now he just had to make sure he got out of the hall unseen. He crept along the gallery, and after inching his way quietly down the stairs he stood for a moment at the door to the hall and took a last look around. Proudly he looked up at the pillar in which his lovingly constructed bomb was hidden. That afternoon the podium would be erected at the base of the pillar, and in the evening, Adolf Hitler would stand on the podium and, like every year, give his speech surrounded by his staff and the big-wigs of the Nazi regime. Georg had hidden enough explosives in the pillar to blow up the hated Führer and all his closest associates. It was too late now to avoid the war in Poland, but Georg was convinced that with his carefully planned assassination he would avert a far greater catastrophe.

He took a deep breath and left the hall, closing the door quietly behind him. He could hear voices from the kitchen as he crept towards the emergency exit at the other end of the corridor. Without making a sound, he squeezed past several boxes and out into the open. Nobody had noticed him. It was still dark, but it wouldn't be long till the first light of dawn. Georg took a gulp of air and savored the cool November air, which quickly washed away his tiredness.

What if by some stroke of bad luck, both clocks stopped? Then all his efforts would have been in vain.

And worse: the Führer would continue to wreak havoc in Germany and the rest of the world. He had already marched into Poland, and Georg was sure the warmongering dictator would also march into France. It was only a question of time until Europe descended into chaos and countless people died.

Georg walked deliberately slowly and nonchalantly across the grounds of the Bürgerbräukeller toward Kellerstraße. He decided to have a cup of coffee at the nearby kiosk before returning to his apartment on Türkenstraße. There he would say goodbye to the carpenter Bróg before catching the next train to Friedrichshafen, where he would catch a ferry to Constance. From there, he would cross the border to Switzerland.

As he stepped onto the sidewalk of Kellerstraße he noticed a man on the other side of the street staring at him. He was wearing a dark-brown leather coat and was of medium height. The man stepped purposefully into the street and started walking toward him. Georg felt his stomach tighten in fear. One look into the eyes of the stranger told him that the man knew. Georg stayed rooted to the spot. Who was this guy? Gestapo? Had they had an eye on him all along and decided to arrest him only now? Had experts already been sent to the hall to defuse the bomb?

"Georg Elser?" The man spoke in a quiet, clear voice. It was more of a statement than a question.

"What do you want?" Georg asked, hoarsely.

"I need to talk to you. Carry on walking. Slowly."

In a daze, Georg set off again, unable to take his eyes off the stranger. He was around forty, with short, blond hair. Those eyes … The man was looking at him like an old friend. Did he know him from somewhere?

"What do you want from me?" Georg repeated.

"I know everything about you," the stranger whispered. "And about your plan. The bomb in the hollowed-out pillar."

Georg could feel panic welling up inside him. The man must be from the Gestapo! They must have been watching him the whole time. But in that case, why hadn't they just arrested him? Did this man want him to confess? He tried lying. "I don't know what you're talking about."

The stranger chuckled softly. "Oh yes, you know exactly what I'm talking about. You don't need to be afraid. I'm not from the Gestapo or the SS."

Georg came to a halt and stared at the man. "Who are you?"

"My name is Max Jung. I'm part of an organization that has a strong interest in your plan succeeding."

Was this man from the resistance? But how could he know about Georg's plan? And if he wanted the plan to succeed, as he claimed, why couldn't he leave Georg in peace? Something wasn't right. His gut feeling told him this conversation shouldn't be taking place. "Where are you from?"

The man smiled. "You would never believe me if I told you, so it's better you don't ask. I just want to help you."

It was so surreal. This man had appeared out of nowhere and was offering to help Georg. Now, when he'd already finished his work. "I don't need any help," he said, and noticed that his voice was trembling.

"Oh yes you do. Because your plan is going to fail."

The plan ... it had become the most important thing in Georg's life these last few months. He had prepared everything meticulously and had even tested his construction in his parents' garden. Now he threw caution to the wind. "My device *will* work," he said, almost offended.

Jung nodded. Then he reached into one of his coat pockets and pulled out two photos. He handed one of them to Georg. He took the photo and recognized the hall of the Bürgerbräukeller. It lay in ruins, the back wall had collapsed, as had the roof. Was this a trick? A forgery? The man handed him the second photo. It showed Adolf Hitler in uniform in front of the Eiffel Tower. Georg shook his head and looked back at the stranger.

"Where did you get these? I don't understand what—"

Jung interrupted him. "Your bomb will work. But Hitler will leave the hall thirteen minutes before it goes off, in order to catch the train back to Berlin. He won't be able to fly tonight because of severe fog."

How did this man know what would happen this evening? How could he know that Munich would be covered in fog that evening? Of course, it was often foggy at this time of year, but ... And where had he got these photos? Was this Jung person mad? It simply didn't make any sense. Georg handed the photos back to him. "What do you want from me?"

Jung took a deep breath and exhaled slowly. "You will now go back into the Bürgerbräukeller. You will reset the timer for nine o'clock."

Georg shook his head. He felt like he was in a bad dream. He shrugged helplessly. "And then?"

"Then Hitler will die this evening and you alone

will have averted immeasurable suffering in Europe and the world."

2

"Strange."

Christoph looked up from his Electronic Flight Bag, the tablet on which he had been reading the approach charts for Frankfurt Airport, and turned to his first officer on the right-hand side of the cockpit. He wasn't particularly worried. Since taking off from New York five hours ago, the flight had gone smoothly. Due to Hurricane Bob off the coast of Newfoundland, they'd taken a more northerly flight route than planned, but otherwise there had been nothing out of the ordinary. The A380 was packed to the last seat, probably due to the many business travelers returning home for the Day of German Unity holiday weekend.

"What's strange?" Christoph asked.

"I just thought I saw a flash of lightning," Daniel Berger said.

Christoph looked at the screen with the weather radar. It was completely black, so there were no heavy clouds. They were about six hundred miles below the southern tip of Greenland and there had been no severe weather warnings for this part of the flight, so it couldn't be a thunderstorm. "Are you sure?"

"No, I only saw it out of the corner of my eye. Maybe the strobe lights of another aircraft?"

It sounded feasible to Christoph. The North Atlantic was a busy flight route. A number of planes could be flying toward Europe close to GH124 on different flight levels. On the other hand, there was no other aircraft to be seen on the navigation display. He leaned forward to look out of the cockpit windows, but all he could see was the blackness of the transatlantic night. He leaned back in his seat. "Maybe a plane whose TCAS isn't functioning. Can't harm to ask." For this part of the flight, Daniel was at the controls, so it was Christoph's job to make contact with the air traffic controllers. They had already passed N56W030 half an hour ago, and were now in the airspace of Shanwick Oceanic. Christoph quickly checked that the correct frequency was set and pressed the push-to-talk button. "Shanwick, GH124 on flight level three fifty. Request information about traffic on NAT Delta."

The answer came immediately, even if the air traffic controller was hard to understand over the rustling of the HF connection. "GH124, Shanwick Oceanic Control. There is no traffic. NAT Delta was closed after you because of the movement of Hurricane Bob. You're the only aircraft in a radius of one hundred and fifty miles."

Christoph and Daniel exchanged brief glances, then Christoph pressed the speaker button again. "Everything OK, Shanwick. No problems. Thanks." He turned to Daniel. "I was wondering why it was so quiet. They must have re-routed all aircraft after us to the south. Aren't you getting tired?" Daniel had just recovered from the flu and although he had been deemed fit to fly, he still looked worse for wear.

"I'm fine. But I could do with a coffee."

Christoph was about to call through to the galley, when he saw it: a pale light, right outside the cockpit window.

"There it is again," Daniel said calmly.

"It isn't lightning, I'm sure of that," Christoph said. It was a ghostly light, and it continued to spread in front of the cockpit windows. Christoph leaned forward again. The whole nose of the plane was shrouded in a pale, whitish aura, as if God had surrounded the aircraft in a halo. Christoph had never seen anything like it.

"That's spooky. What do you think it is?" Daniel asked.

"I think it's St. Elmo's Fire."

"But we're hundreds of miles from the nearest thundercloud."

Christoph checked the aircraft systems. Speed, temperature, pressure—there was nothing to indicate a problem. "I don't get it, either. Everything seems to be OK."

The light grew stronger as the minutes passed, until it was almost dazzling. Christoph remembered a documentary he had seen a few weeks ago on the Discovery Channel about the space shuttle. On re-entry into the Earth's atmosphere it had been surrounded by a bright plasma column. This here looked exactly the same—as if the A380 had been in space and was now reentering Earth's atmosphere. He shook his head as he was jolted out of his reverie by the buzzing of the intercom phone, which showed that one of the flight attendants wanted to talk to him. He picked up the receiver.

"Wilder, what's up?"

As soon as she answered, Christoph recognized Veronica's voice. She was a damned good-looking blonde, and sharp as a tack, too. She was the purser on today's flight.

"Captain, we have some smoke in the cabin at U2Left."

"Smoke?" He repeated the word, so that his co-pilot, who had put his interphone on quiet, could also hear what was going on. "Where exactly?"

"On the whole upper deck. It seems to be coming from the ventilation system. I've already ordered a search for the cause."

"Thanks, Veronica. Keep me updated."

"And another thing, Christoph: the wings appear to be surrounded by a pale light; the outboard engines, too."

Now Christoph was starting to feel nervous. The St. Elmo's Fire appeared to be surrounding the whole plane, and added to that was the smoke, which every pilot's worst nightmare. There must be a connection between the two. But what? He re-checked the systems. Everything still appeared to be fine, until his eyes fell on the engine display. He didn't like what he saw one bit. "The EGT of one and four is going up," he said out loud. Something was going on, but he had no idea what.

"Do you have an idea? What do you think?" he asked his first officer. It wasn't a sign of weakness— every good pilot involved his team in dealing with problems.

But Daniel shook his head. "I don't know."

Suddenly Christoph felt a slight juddering, as if they were flying through an area of light turbulence, but he knew instinctively that the vibration wasn't coming from the atmosphere.

"Now the EGT of two and three is also rising. And the thrust of one and four is also going up slightly."

The engines were controlled by the autothrust. There was nothing unusual about the computer changing the thrust when wind conditions changed, but Christoph was fairly sure it was another symptom of the imminent problem.

Enough was enough! "I have control," Christoph said loudly and clearly to his first officer. There should never be any doubt in the cockpit as to who was in charge of the aircraft.

"You have control!" Daniel confirmed. For the next few minutes, nothing else happened. The A380 was still flying on autopilot. But if it became necessary, Christoph would have to take the controls. It was only logical: he was the highest-ranking pilot in the cockpit and had considerably more experience than his copilot. Christoph studied the engine display again and shook his head in disbelief as his gaze fell on the numbers of the exhaust gas temperature. The temperature in all four engines was rising steadily. Whatever the problem was, it must be coming from outside the aircraft, otherwise all four engines wouldn't be affected. Or was something wrong with the fuel? No, that couldn't be it. The stuff was so well mixed—if that was the problem, it would have been apparent soon after takeoff. His eyes wandered to the cockpit windows, which flickered in the ghostly light of the St. Elmo's Fire. He tried to think back to his pilot training. St. Elmo's Fire was caused by the exchange of electrical charges on the aircraft cladding and was pretty rare in air traffic. Electrically charged particles in the atmosphere were usually responsible.

Electrically charged particles?

Something in his head went *click* and he felt his heart skip a beat. My God!

"The volcano!" Christoph murmured.

"Christoph?" Daniel asked.

"The volcano!" Christoph looked at Daniel, whose eyes were widening. "We've flown into a cloud of

17

volcanic ash."

"Here? The Eyjafjalla … whatever it's called, sent a cloud over the Baltic Sea and Scandinavia. We're hundreds of miles away from the no-fly zone."

Daniel was right. They hadn't been given a NOTAM in the briefing, either, since their route wasn't supposed to take them anywhere near the ash cloud. And in any case, the most recent eruption had been considerably weaker than the one that had paralyzed air traffic in 2010. But what else could be causing the St. Elmo's Fire and the irregularities in the engine data? And if they were flying through an ash cloud, they needed to make sure they got out of it as quickly as possible. Christoph initiated a 180 degree turn with the heading knob. Immediately the aircraft started to turn around in a wide arc.

"Daniel: ask the controller about the volcanic ash situation over the Atlantic, and request a change to our flight altitude. I better switch on the fasten seatbelt sign."

Christoph reached up above his head and flipped the switch in the overhead panel. Daniel hadn't even started to speak when the Master Caution alarm wailed through the cockpit. "Eng1 Flameout," Christoph read on the engine display.

"Engine one is spooling down," the first officer said in a calm voice. The moment Christoph looked at the screen, the other three engines shut down. "Two, three and four are also spooling down," he said. The engine RPMs were falling rapidly. When they fell below the critical point, the lights went out in the cockpit. Only the most important displays remained active.

"All Engine Flameout. We are in battery mode,"

Daniel confirmed.

Christoph nodded grimly. It briefly flashed through his mind that it was strange he wasn't starting to panic, but he had been well trained for this kind of situation. He remembered the hours he had spent in the flight simulator not so long ago. "Checklist!"

"It's already on the screen. Speed two hundred and fifty knots."

Christoph turned the speed knob on the autopilot and checked the settings. At two hundred and fifty knots they would have the lowest sink rate. "Two hundred and fifty knots set."

"Autothrust off."

"Autothrust is off."

Step by step they went through the checklist.

"Thrust lever idle."

Christoph reached for the thrust levers on the center console and set them back to idle."

"Thrust is at idle."

Daniel ticked off the point on the screen by pressing the corresponding button on the console. Christoph had hoped the air flow through the engine would start up the turbines again by windmilling, but nothing happened.

"That's it for now. Once we've passed flight level two hundred, we'll try to restart with the APU."

Christoph checked the sinkrate. They were falling one thousand five hundred feet per minute. At the moment they were at a height of over thirty-five thousand feet, meaning they had twenty minutes left.

"How far is it to the next airport?" Christoph knew it was in Ireland.

"Shannon. Five hundred miles," Daniel replied. There was now a hint of panic in his voice. That was way too far.

"Set a course!"

"One hundred and twelve degrees."

Christoph looked at the display in front of him. He corrected the flight direction using the heading knob on the AFS. The St. Elmo's Fire was still flimmering in front of the cockpit windows, so they must still be in the cloud of volcanic ash. If the ash particles had really clogged the engines, they had to get out of this cloud. Otherwise, they'd never be able to restart the turbines. If they weren't already so clogged with ash they were gone for good, that was. Christoph knew that with the waves of the North Atlantic, they had no chance of landing the huge aircraft smoothly on the surface of the water. It would break apart at first contact. The wings would be torn off, the cabin would overturn and the wreckage, with the passengers still strapped in their seats, would sink like a stone.

Christoph wiped the sweat from his brow. He mustn't think about it. If he started to panic they would never get through this.

He glanced to his left. Daniel was looking agitatedly from one instrument to the next and mumbling something.

"Speak up."

Daniel looked straight at him. His eyes were red. "I said, if we can't restart the engines, we've had it!"

Christoph laid a hand gently on Daniel's shoulder. "Nobody is going to die today. Yes, the situation is critical, but if we keep a clear head, we have a better chance of getting through this than if we panic." He let his words sink in. "And I need your help, OK?"

It took several long seconds, but finally Daniel nodded. "OK." The first officer breathed deeply in and out.

"We're going to go through the checklist, OK?" Maybe this would calm Daniel down a little.

"OK," Daniel answered tonelessly. He looked at the instruments in front of him. "Passing flight level three hundred and thirty."

"Report to Shanwick."

"OK. Shanwick Oceanic, GI124. Mayday, Mayday, Mayday. Complete engine flameout. I repeat. All four engines have failed. Probable cause, volcanic ash."

"GI124, Shanwick Oceanic, emergency declared at Zulu 0445, complete engine failure. Confirm your position, course, flight level and persons on board." The voice of the controller was difficult to hear over the rustling.

Daniel hesitated a moment and looked at the screen. "Just passing flight level three hundred and twenty. Position N56W025. Course one hundred and twelve. We are trying to reach Shannon if we are able to restart a couple of the engines. Windmilling has failed so far."

"Copy that, GI124. We don't have you on the radar yet. Informing Shannon."

Now Christoph noticed an unpleasant smell. Sulfur. He sniffed loudly and turned around, but in the darkness he could see hardly anything. He reached for the flashlight to the left of his seat, switched it on and immediately saw trails of smoke wafting through the cockpit. "We have …" His sentence was interrupted by another alarm signal. He looked at the status display.

"Cabin pressure is going down. Probably because of the flameout," Daniel said.

Christoph nodded. The air in the cabin was

supplied from compressed air in the engines. If they weren't running, the pressure in the cabin inevitably went down. "Oxygen masks on."

He reached to the left of his seat again and pulled out the oxygen mask. When he let go of the red valves, it adhered to his face. Finally he put on the headset with the microphone.

Daniel had put on his mask at the same time. Christoph could hear the hissing of the regulator in his ears.

"I'm going to make a passenger announcement." He pressed the button on the center console and spoke without thinking about what he was going to say. "This is the Captain speaking. I'm sure you have noticed that we are experiencing some engine trouble. This has probably been caused by volcanic ash, and is causing loss of pressure in the cabin. For this reason we are activating the oxygen masks which will fall from above your heads shortly. We are doing all we can to restart the engines. We have the aircraft under control and are able to maneuver it. We are well trained for exactly this kind of situation and will solve the problem. Please follow the instructions of the flight attendants. We will keep you updated on our progress." He released the button and hoped that all hell wouldn't break loose in the cabin.

"That was a major understatement," Daniel commented darkly.

Christoph shrugged. He reached up to the console above his head, opened the red protective lid, hesitated a moment, and pressed the button. Now the oxygen masks would drop from the ceiling in the cabin. He didn't want to picture what was going on among the hundreds of passengers. Here in the cockpit, they were completely cut off the back—but they had enough on their hands.

"Passing flight level two hundred and fifty," Daniel said.

The sound of the Master Caution penetrated even through the headphones. Christoph tore his eyes away from the display and looked out of the window. St. Elmo's Fire was still flickering. He shook his head. He had anticipated that the unexpected volcanic ash would appear in a narrow altitude range. Why on earth hadn't the meteorologists noticed this westward-moving cloud? What the hell had gone wrong?

Apart from the pale light in front of the cabin windows there was nothing but endless darkness outside. No stars, no horizon. At this time of year they would only expect to see the sun rise shortly before landing in Frankfurt. If they had to ditch the plane, Christoph didn't even stand a chance of seeing the movement of the waves in order to approach the water at the best possible angle.

His eyes kept flicking back to the altimeter. They were passing twenty-five thousand feet. About another four minutes until they reached flight level two hundred. Then the outside pressure would be high enough to try and start the APU. Once the Auxiliary Power Unit was running, they could try to restart the main engines. Until then they could only hope that windmilling would get the engine blades back up and running, but since that hadn't happened yet, Christoph was not particularly optimistic.

The waiting and the inaction were nerve-wracking, and Christoph struggled to stem the panic welling up inside him. During his career as a pilot he had mastered several critical situations, but he had never even dared to imagine complete engine failure over the North Atlantic. He remembered there'd been a plane a couple of years ago that had run out of kerosene over the Atlantic. Luckily, the pilots had been able to execute a glide landing on the Azores. But here there was nothing but water far and wide. They had enough fuel, but what use was that when the engines were clogged with volcanic ash? They had to restart at least two of them. Somehow!

Three more minutes!

"I'm going check the situation out back," Christoph said. Daniel nodded.

Veronica answered his call. She was breathing heavily, as she probably wasn't wearing her oxygen mask the whole time so she could speak to passengers.

"How's it going in the cabin?"

"We have a medical emergency in Business. Elderly man. Cardiac arrest. Reanimation with the defibrillator. I didn't want to disturb you and asked for a doctor over the PA. A doctor is trying to stabilize him."

"OK, good work. And otherwise? The passengers?"

"The passengers are in their seats and reasonably calm, but very frightened. Some of the oxygen masks in Economy aren't working, but those people are sharing their masks with their neighbors."

"OK. Thanks Veronica."

"Christoph?"

"Yes?"

"Will the engines restart?" Her voice was calm, which was no doubt the result of her many years of flying and rigorous training, but Christoph was sure the experienced crew were also afraid. Veronica knew exactly what would happen if they couldn't restart the engines.

Christoph breathed deeply. "We're doing our best." What else could he say? It was doubtful if the ash-clogged turbines would ever work again. Should he lie?

In any case, it wasn't the answer Veronica had been hoping for. "Understood, Christoph." But her voice remained calm.

"Veronica?"

"Yes?"

"Chin up!" he said, and broke off the connection without waiting for an answer.

"Flight level two hundred and ten!" Daniel reported. One minute, then they would know.

"OK. We're going to proceed strictly according to the checklist."

"Understood."

Daniel's gaze was fixed on the altimeter on the display in front of him and he counted down in his head.

Twenty thousand four hundred feet.

Twenty thousand three hundred feet.

Please, please!

Twenty thousand two hundred feet.

He took a quick look at the checklist on the center console to internalize the necessary steps, although Daniel would read out and tick off the numbers one by one.

Twenty thousand one hundred feet.

Christoph tried to keep breathing regularly.

"Flight level two hundred!" Daniel said.

"Let's go," Christoph said.

"APU start!"

Christoph pressed the main APU switch on the ceiling panel to activate the electronics. Immediately, a new alarm sound reverberated through the cockpit. He'd expected this. The APU flap wasn't designed for this kind of speed. But to hell with it! They needed the APU. "APU switched on."

"Now wait two minutes for it to start."

Christoph nodded. He looked out of the cockpit windows: they were still surrounded by the eerie light, so clearly hadn't left the cloud of volcanic ash. Hopefully the stuff wouldn't also ruin the APU! He stared at the timer as if he could make it move faster through sheer force of will.

After several torturous seconds the APU finally booted up and the lights came on in the cockpit. It was a good sign but still their fate depended on the four engines beneath the wings.

The two minutes were finally up.

"All main engine switches off," Daniel read out the next point on the checklist.

Christoph flipped the switch on the center console. "All off!"

"Wing Anti Ice off!"

"Wing Anti Ice off!"

"APU Bleed on!

"APU Bleed on!"

"Engine Master 2 on!" Daniel said huskily.

Now it was critical.

"Engine Master 2 on," said Christoph and flipped the big square switch.

He looked at the RPM display.

"Come on!" Daniel cried.

Nothing happened. "It's not working. Try number three!" Christoph turned off two and activated three. Negative!

"Fucking useless!" Daniel swore.

"Calm down!" Christoph said. He tried switching between the individual engines, but nothing happened.

"We're already down to ten thousand feet."

"I can see that. At least we're out of the ash cloud. The St. Elmo's Fire is gone."

"That doesn't change the fact that we'll be swimming in the Atlantic in seven minutes."

Christoph didn't answer.

"Or diving, rather!" Daniel added grimly. Christoph kept trying to start the individual engines.

They were still going down fifteen hundred feet per minute. It was no use, Christoph told himself. They had to accept that the engines were gone. A ditch was now unavoidable. However slim the chances of survival were, he would do everything in his power to land on the water as gently as possible. He pressed the button for the cabin loudspeaker. "Cabin crew, prepare for emergency water landing."

Nine thousand feet. Less than two miles separated them from the icy water of the North Atlantic. If only they were flying in daylight, he would at least be able to see the surface of the water!

Suddenly there was a hard jolt. The whole aircraft was vibrating.

"Turbulence!" Christoph said.

"As if it wasn't bad enough!"

The vibrations got worse. An empty coffee cup skittered across the floor behind him.

"I hope this doesn't carry on till we land!" Daniel

said loudly.

It would be difficult to keep the wings straight with all this juddering. Another powerful jolt rocked the aircraft as if it had been struck by wind shears.

"What the …" Daniel began.

Between the shaking, Christoph noticed a barely discernible but familiar vibration. His eyes fell on the right-hand display in front of him. He could hardly believe his eyes.

"Number four is starting!" he cried.

They passed eight thousand feet and as suddenly as the turbulence had started, it was gone. Now Christoph could clearly feel the vibrations of an engine starting up.

"My God, I don't believe it," Daniel whispered.

"I didn't reckon with that," Christoph admitted. The thrust of number four stabilized. He pulled lightly on the sidestick and slowed the rate of descent. But they still wouldn't make it to Shannon.

"We're still going down, just more slowly. Six thousand feet," Daniel said. "One isn't enough. What's with the others?"

"We'll find out in a minute," Christoph replied and stretched out his hand. He tried to activate one of the inner engines. Number two.

"It's coming!" Daniel shouted. "It's starting up!"

Christoph watched the RPM of engine two slowly go up on the screen. The descent rate dropped to zero, then the aircraft started to slowly, ponderously ascend.

"My God, we're going up!" Daniel groaned. He laughed out of sheer relief. "We're really going up!"

When engine two reached eighty percent thrust, a strong vibration penetrated the airframe. The engine must be damaged. Christoph saw that the RPM was fluctuating. At the same time, the exhaust temperature of the engine was rising rapidly, nearing the red zone.

"Two must have been hit bad. We have an instable combustion." Christoph called through to the cabin crew. Veronica picked up immediately.

"Please look out of the window at two and tell me what you can see."

A few seconds passed before the chief flight attendant answered: "Flames are coming out of the engine. But it looks undamaged from the outside. The passengers at the window are extremely worried."

Christoph wasn't surprised. "It looks worse than it is. The engine isn't getting enough air, which is why the combustion is instable. At least we were able to stop sinking. I just hope the two engines hold out. But first of all, please reassure the passengers. What's happened to the medical emergency?"

"The man died. The doctor wasn't able to stabilize him."

Christoph closed his eyes for a second. Now, under his command, a man had died during an emergency situation. Although he didn't think they could have done anything differently, he still felt guilty. He pushed the thought aside. It was a long way to Shannon and if number two didn't hold out, they would inevitably start sinking again. He would have to deal with his feelings later. "Thank you, Veronica." He ended the conversation and turned to Daniel. "How far to Shannon?"

"Three-hundred miles. At our current speed a bit less than an hour. I'll inform Shanwick."

"OK."

While Daniel spoke with the air traffic controllers,

Christoph checked the status of the engines. The N1 of number two was still fluctuating wildly, and the exhaust temperature had already activated the alarm. Christoph took the thrust lever and shifted it down to seventy percent. RPM and temperature stabilized, but the aircraft did not ascend anymore. They were flying at an altitude of seven thousand feet, and if another engine didn't miraculously spring to life, they would have to remain at this altitude. The air traffic controller advised them to fly directly toward Shannon. The airport had already been alerted about the imminent emergency landing.

"It's still pitch dark outside," Christoph murmured. "What's the local time in Shannon?"

"Five thirteen. So we'll land around six local time. If the engines hold out, that is. I don't understand why two and four are running, but not the others."

"We have to make it to Shannon, then a technician will be able to tell us why." Christoph looked at the display. "We should dump fuel as soon as possible. Can you deal with that?"

Daniel nodded and got to work. They needed less fuel to get to Shannon than to Frankfurt. By dumping the excess fuel they would also reduce their weight and get more speed from the damaged engines.

Time passed, and Christoph and Daniel exchanged hardly a word. Number four was running stably and two also seemed to be holding out. The pilots tried repeatedly to restart one and three, but without success. Finally the air traffic controller reported that he had their plane on the radar, and told Christoph and Daniel to make contact with Shannon.

"I'll switch Shannon Approach on 121.4. Shannon Approach, GH124."

"GH124, Shannon Approach. I've been informed of your situation. I have you at fifty miles distance. We've reserved Runway zero-six for you. There's no wind and visibility is excellent. Take course one hundred and head for Foynes, from there for the ILS approach zero-six, frequency 109.5, air pressure QNH 1007."

"Shannon, copy that. Via Foynes, clearance for ILS approach zero-six, winds understood, QNH 1007," Daniel confirmed.

"GH124, now switch to Tower 118.7"

Christoph changed the frequency to the value they had been given. A glance at the navigation display showed him they were nearing the Irish coast. He leaned forward in his seat and looked out of the window. Yes, he could see the lights of some villages on the coast. Down there to the right must be Kilkee and beyond it Kilrush on the Shannon Estuary.

"Not far now. I think we're going to make it," Daniel murmured.

"Don't say it too loudly. The thrust on two is fluctuating again," Christoph responded.

"You're right, damn it. And the exhaust temperature is rising again. Fuck. It's got to hold out these last few minutes."

They flew over the Shannon Estuary and according to instructions, reduced their flight altitude to three thousand feet. Shortly before they reached the beacon they were aiming for, Shannon Approach reported over the radio.

"GH124. Head straight for course zero-six-zero. Confirm ILS."

They had received the signal from the instrument landing system a few minutes ago. "Confirm ILS

Runway zero-six."

Christoph was now flying the aircraft manually, and started to turn it round for the approach.

"There it is!" Daniel cried. "There's the runway. Runway in sight!"

Christoph could also make out the two-mile-long strip illuminated by approach lights. He flew the aircraft straight ahead until they were just in front of the runway.

"Gear down."

Daniel put the landing gear lever to his left down. The lights changed from red to green. "Landing gear is down."

Christoph felt a hefty vibration and immediately his eyes fell on the engine display. "The thrust of number two is fluctuating very strongly. We have to prepared for it switching off at any moment. Flaps on two."

"Flaps two." Daniel pulled the lever back.

There was a short peeping sound. "Outer marker. Another five miles," Daniel said.

They crossed the Shannon estuary again. Christoph could see the lights of the town directly beyond the runway. There was a big jolt, then engine two shut down completely.

"Shit! Flaps three!" After a few seconds they were already below the glideslope, as he could see from the three red lights of the VASI. Christoph pushed the thrust lever of the only still-functioning engine as far as it would go. He had to push the rudder almost completely to the right in order to compensate for the torque. He couldn't stop the descend and he knew that they would touch down before the start of the runway.

"How much further?" Christoph asked.

"Three point five miles."

A sing-song male voice came from the radio altimeter: "one thousand!"

"Checked!" Christoph and Daniel replied in unison.

"Landing checklist!" Christoph said.

"Landing checklist," Daniel confirmed. "ECAM memo landing. No blue!"

Christoph pulled the sidestick further and further back to maintain the sink rate of nine hundred feet per minute. He was swearing under his breath. The landing weight was much too high, making the aircraft as stubborn as an overweight mule.

"Five hundred," bleated the acoustic system, announcing their altitude.

"For Christ's sake, it's got to manage these last few feet!" Daniel swore.

"Calm down!" Christoph said quietly. He concentrated on the runway.

"Four hundred."

Now the last light on the VASI changed to red. They were far too low. What was the saying? *Red and red and soon you're dead!*

"Three hundred."

They had done everything they could. Now he could only hope that the ground in front of the runway was strong enough to carry this bird.

"Two hundred."

The runway was now right in front of them.

"One hundred."

Christoph pulled the sidestick back even further.

"Fifty."

The sink rate went down. Maybe they would make

it after all.

"Retard … retard … retard!" came from the automated warning system. The sink rate dropped to almost zero. A wind must have whipped up close to the ground. Right at the end of the touchdown zone, the main landing gear touched the ground of the runway.

"It's possible to have a bit of luck sometimes," Christoph murmured quietly. Hurriedly he pulled the thrust lever back, but avoided giving any counterthrust. Who knew how the engine would react? And in any case, the runway was long enough to brake slowly.

"I don't believe it. We're down. And in one piece!" Daniel let out a gasp of air.

"Did you doubt it?"

"Honestly? Yes."

"GH124, Shannon Approach. Good landing! Can you leave the runway?"

The first officer looked at Christoph. He gave a brief nod.

"Thank you, Shannon," Daniel said. "We lost another engine during our approach and only have one functioning engine, but we can leave the runway via a high-speed exit. We need medical assistance because of a drop in pressure and unfortunately we have a dead passenger."

"Good, leave zero-six via D2 and stop there next to the hangar. Ground crew and medical assistance are already waiting. And the fire service."

"Understood. Leaving zero-six via D2. Thank you, Shannon."

The aircraft reached the end of the runway and almost came to a standstill. Christoph reduced the pressure on the brakes and turned off onto the adjoining taxiway. They crossed a disused runway, and finally reached the hangar specified by the controller. Fire engines and ambulances were already there, and two mobile gangways and several buses approached them from the other side of the apron.

Slowly Christoph pressed his foot down on the pedal until the aircraft came to a stop next to the emergency services.

"Leave the fasten seatbelt sign on, I'll make an announcement," he said to Daniel. The first officer nodded.

Christoph put on the parking brake while Daniel spoke to the cabin crew over the PA: "Cabin crew, all doors in park!"

On the screen, Christoph watched all the doors being set to open, so that they didn't activate the emergency slides when opened. Only then did he switch off the last engine. He leaned back in his seat, closed his eyes for a moment and breathed deeply. Then he reached for the cabin phone.

"This is the captain speaking. We have made it through a challenging situation and have made a safe intermediate landing in Shannon. I know the last ninety minutes have been very difficult for you, and would like to thank you for following the instructions of our cabin crew so courageously. Please remain seated for a few more minutes until the stairs have been docked to the main deck. Passenger buses are waiting outside to take you to the airport building. Thank you for your cooperation."

He nodded to Daniel. "Fasten seatbelt signs off."

"Nice speech," said his first officer and flipped the switch. A loud "ping" resounded through the cockpit.

Christoph could feel his adrenalin level slowly going down. Gradually he became aware of how critical the situation had been and how narrowly they had all escaped with their lives. If they hadn't been able to restart the engines, they would now be lying dead on the floor of the Atlantic. Or they would have crashed to the ground if the last engine had given out any earlier.

He looked his first officer in the eye and reached out a hand. Daniel grasped it with trembling fingers. Then they turned their attention to the checklist for switching off the aircraft systems.

"Did we do everything correctly?" Daniel asked.

Christoph knew what his colleague was getting at. There would be an investigation which would take months, and which would analyze the actions of the crew precisely. If they were found to be responsible in any way, it could damage their careers irreparably, especially as the incident had resulted in one death.

The dead man … Christoph had almost suppressed the news. He sighed, unbuckled his seatbelt and pushed his seat back.

"OK. I'll go into the cabin."

Daniel nodded as he packed up his things.

Christoph stood up, went to the back of the cockpit and opened the door. He climbed down the few steps, past the flight crew rest compartment and opened the second door to the lower of the two cabin levels.

He came just in time to see the last passengers leave the aircraft. An elderly, gray-haired man in a creased suit gave him a curt nod when he saw Christoph in his pilot's uniform and murmured a hardly audible "Thank you."

Gaby, a tall, red-haired flight attendant who always wore a little too much make-up, said goodbye to the final passenger and turned to Christoph. "That was pretty close, wasn't it?"

Christoph nodded, but did not volunteer and further information. "Where's the dead passenger?"

Gaby stepped closer and indicated with a brief wave of the hand toward the stairs. "Upstairs at the front of Business. The paramedics and the doctor were only there briefly. There was nothing they could do. Veronica is with him and his wife."

Christoph nodded again, patted Gaby on the arm and climbed the stairs to the upper deck. As he went up he could already hear suppressed sobs. On reaching the top of the stairs, he saw the deceased passenger a few rows away. He was sitting upright in his seat at the window, a blanket covering his upper body but not his face. The man's mouth was open, as if he had tried in vain to get a last gasp of air; his eyes stared blankly. He was probably in his mid-seventies. Next to him was sitting a slim woman with carefully groomed short gray wavy hair. Tears were running down her cheeks and forming dark spots on her beige blouse. Her right hand rested trembling on her husband's hand, which was still gripping the armrest. Veronica was kneeling beside the woman and rubbing her shoulders.

As Christoph approached, the old woman looked up at him with puffed-up eyes. Christoph had to swallow. Did she hold him responsible for her husband's death? There was nothing he could have done to prevent the flight through the ash cloud. But had he reacted in the right way? He would find out in the investigation. But regardless of what the investigation revealed, a man had died during an emergency situation on board under his command and he knew this would haunt him for the rest of his life. The man was dead and nothing that Christoph did would bring him back to life. Here and now he could only try to stay composed and accept responsibility, however unpleasant the situation was. He kneeled down beside the woman until he was face to face. "I am the captain, Christoph Wilder," he said calmly. "I am terribly sorry about the death of your husband."

The woman sobbed. "What happened up there?"

"We flew into a cloud of volcanic ash. The ash clogged the engines, which then switched off. We were able to restart two of the engines, but in the meantime we lost pressure and the cabin filled with smoke."

"My husband suddenly started gasping for air …" The woman sobbed again. "He grabbed at his chest just before the lights went out. When they went back on he was … he was …" Her voice broke.

"The doctor said Mr. Prandtl had a cardiac arrest," Veronica said quietly while stroking the woman's arm. "Possibly caused by the loss of pressure or difficulty breathing because of the smoke."

Christoph nodded slowly. He waited until Mrs. Prandtl had calmed down a little. "I know this is no consolation for you now, but the airline will take good care of you. A minster is already on the way here." He hoped this was true. As soon as he could, he would talk to the handling agent and station manager about it. He took a deep breath. "And I am also personally at your disposal whenever you need me, Mrs. Prandtl."

The woman looked up and her eyes narrowed a little. "You personally?" She sniffed again, but the tone of her voice had hardened. "And will that bring him back to life?"

Christoph swallowed.

He searched for the right words, but Mrs. Prandtl continued: "In two weeks we wanted to celebrate his eightieth birthday together. Now he's dead!"

She wiped the tears from her eyes and gave Christoph a hostile look. What he had feared had come to pass: she was making him responsible for her husband's death.

"Mrs. Prandtl, I can assure you ..."

"You can assure me of nothing, Captain. My husband is dead. He is dead. And you and your airline are responsible for his death."

"Ssshhh ..." Veronica tried to soothe her.

Mrs. Prandtl glanced at her briefly and pushed her hand from her shoulder before turning back to Christoph. "Go, Captain! You have no business being here."

"I ..." Christoph began, but he could see there was no point. He stood up, turned around slowly and left, while behind him Mrs. Prandtl resumed her sobbing. Feeling numb, he went back down the steps to the lower deck. He barely noticed two women from the Red Cross running past him up the stairs.

3

"I think I'm dying!"

Hearing Erika's words, Herbert felt his stomach tighten.

"You're not dying!" He wanted to sound upbeat, but all that came out of his mouth was a guttural rasping noise. He didn't even manage a smile. Resigned, he removed the damp flannel from his wife's forehead and dipped it in the bucket of water, which he had filled that morning at the well near the entrance to the bunker. Then the water had still been cold, now it was lukewarm. He squeezed some of the water out of the flannel and placed it gently back on her head. Tenderly he stroked her sunken face.

"I'm so cold," she said in a trembling voice.

"Shall I get you another blanket?" Herbert asked softly.

She nodded. "Please."

Herbert stood up and went over to the narrow metal cupboard. A few threadbare pieces of clothing were neatly folded on the bottom shelf, further up was a pillow cover full of holes, but no blanket.

Herbert turned around. "There's nothing here. I'll have to go to the storeroom."

His wife shook her head. "No. Please! Don't leave me alone. Stay with me."

Herbert walked back slowly to the bed. He stooped over her emaciated body and tenderly stroked her gray, matted hair. "It'll only take a few minutes, then I'll be back," he said gently.

"No!" Erika's once so strong voice was devoid of any strength now. When she had said "No" in the past, nobody had dared to contradict her. Now it was just a pathetic whimper.

"You're shivering. I can see how you're freezing. I'll go to the storeroom and get another blanket. I'll be back in five minutes."

She didn't have the energy to argue with him. She closed her eyes and turned her head to the side.

Herbert kissed her tenderly on the cheek and walked to the door. He decided not to turn off the light. His wife hated being in the dark. Even at night he left the door of the bedroom open a crack to let in the light from the hall.

He walked past the doors of other bedrooms that had been abandoned years ago. After a good thirty feet, the corridor forked. Herbert passed the entrance to the rec room and kitchen, then the bathrooms and the small office rooms. After another fifty feet or so he reached a door, which had the word "Storeroom" written on it in flaking white paint. The door was stuck again, possibly because of the cold, and he kicked it open.

The storeroom contained long rows of shelves, most of which were now empty. Flickering neon tube lights bathed the room in a ghostly light. Herbert rifled through three cupboards, and finally found what he was looking for. He took the brown blanket and left the storeroom. On his way back, he passed the little infirmary and hesitated. Most of the medicine cupboards were empty already, but maybe he would find something that would help his wife.

The neon lights flickered into life. In the middle of the room was an operating table next to several rolling containers containing medical instruments. Against the back wall were a desk and the medicine cabinets. Herbert rummaged through the packets of tablets and ampules, whose use-by date had long since passed. Most of the names were unfamiliar to him. He wasn't a doctor and had no idea what might help. But maybe he would find something to relieve the pain.

In the second cabinet he found several vials of morphine in a box, but he didn't know how to use them. There were no instructions to go with them. If Erika's pains got worse, he would simply try a small dose. Herbert put two vials and two syringes in his jacket pocket, then searched through the third cabinet but didn't find anything useful. When he got back to Erika's room, all was quiet. Perhaps she had fallen asleep. Herbert was relieved—then he could have a little rest himself. He crept up to the bed and wanted to spread the additional blanket over his wife when he gave a start. Erika's face was completely relaxed, although she was usually agitated and groaned in her sleep. Then he noticed that her eyes were half open and had a dull sheen.

Herbert dropped the blanket, and a scream rose up in his throat. He dropped to his knees and took her face in both hands. It was strangely cool. "Wake up!" he cried.

No reaction. His wife was dead.

He slumped down by the bed and began to cry bitterly, his hands gripping the bedspread.

4

"Shit!" The constant beeping and a glance at the rearview camera display made it abundantly clear that the parking space was too small for his SUV. All the technology in the world couldn't help him this time. Resigned, he gently stepped on the gas and maneuvered back onto the street.

He had neither a garage nor a permanent parking space in front of his house, and with the lack of parking in this part of Wiesbaden, he would probably have to walk a long way from his car to his front door. As he drove through the narrow streets searching in vain for a parking space, he was overcome by a surge of irritation that he had put off buying a new car for so long. But he liked his spacious SUV and the high seat, which gave him a good overview of the street. He remembered his last vacation with Elena, when they had driven this very car along the picturesque roads above Lake Garda looking for a secluded, romantic restaurant. They had finally found one, with a fantastic view of the lake. Two lighted candles on the table and a delicious dry red wine—it had been the last time they had eaten out together. Now Elena was dead. There would never be another vacation together and this damn SUV was too big for him alone.

Finally he found a parking spot that was big enough. He parked the car and set off on foot back to his house, which was several blocks away.

As the drizzle turned into proper rain, Christoph pulled up his hood. The gray weather and sharp drop in temperature meant that winter was finally on its way. Up to the end of October, it had still been unseasonably warm.

The modern, white house came into view after the next turning and he rummaged in his pocket for the keys. The house was nestled picturesquely in the foothills of the Taunus mountains. Elena had always gushed to her friends that in their garden the lowlands of the Rhine-Main region ended and the Mittelgebirge mountain range began. Now the garden that his wife had so lovingly tended was overgrown with weeds. And just like the car, the house was much too big for him alone.

Christoph stepped inside. He slung his black windbreaker onto the chair in the hall. In the living room, he laid his suit jacket carefully over the arm of the couch. It mustn't get crumpled. He would need it again tomorrow for the next round of the hearing.

In the kitchen he took a bottle of Coke out of the fridge before returning to the living room, where he slumped down into one of the white leather armchairs. The whole week he had struggled through discussions with people from the BFU—the German Federal Bureau of Aircraft Accident Investigation. The inquiry into the incident three weeks ago was well underway. The people who worked at the BFU were polite, matter-of-fact, and professional, but it hadn't escaped Christoph's notice that they systematically picked at his statements looking for weak spots, as if they wanted to make him partially responsible. The incident had received quite a lot of media attention after a well-known pop singer, who had been flying in Business Class, talked to the tabloids about her "near death experience." Christoph had never heard of the woman, but he was more of a Blues man himself.

He and his first officer might just as easily have

been celebrated as heroes who had managed to land the plane and averted a catastrophe. But the old man had died and now they were looking for someone to blame. His superiors had grounded Christoph for the time being and he felt useless and ostracized.

He took a big swig from the bottle and closed his eyes. It was quiet in his house. Much too quiet. When Elena had been alive there had always been music playing. His wife had liked classical music and her impressive collection of CDs now sat untouched on the black shelf next to the TV. The lack of music made Christoph painfully aware that he was all alone. Of course he knew he only had to go over to the shelf, pull out an album and put it in the player, but it didn't seem right. It had been Elena's music and not his; it wouldn't be the same.

He emptied the bottle, picked up the phone and dialed his son's number. He had tried several times over the last few days but nobody had picked up, and even though he'd left his son a message to call him back, the call never came. Not that he'd really expected it.

"Hello?" the clear voice of a woman sounded through the earpiece.

Well, something at least.

"Hi, Andrea." Christoph tried to sound friendly despite the fact that he and his daughter-in-law were barely on speaking terms. "Christoph here. How are you guys doing?"

His question was followed by a moment's silence and he feared she would hang up.

"Hi." Unlike him, Andrea didn't even attempt a friendly tone of voice. "We're fine."

"How's Paul?" It suddenly struck Christoph with a

pang that he hadn't seen his grandson in nearly half a year. And it had been only the third time he had ever seen Paul, who was now two years old.

"Also fine," Andrea answered curtly. "What do you want, Christoph?"

He took a deep breath. There was no point trying to engage in small talk with Andrea. That would probably never change. And it was his fault—his alone. "Is Michael at home?"

"Yes, I'll ask him if he's got time."

While he waited, Christoph heard a child laughing in the background. His grandson! How he wished Michael would simply invite him over for a visit. He pictured himself jumping into the car and speeding down the expressway to Heidelberg. Imagined lifting Paul up in his arms, giving him a big hug and ruffling his fuzzy blonde hair. He would buy him a big toy plane and play with him in the garden.

"What do you want?" The sound of his son's voice ripped him out of his daydream. The hostility in his voice was impossible to ignore. Christoph could be grateful that his son had come to the phone at all.

"I ... I just wanted to hear how you all are."

"Can't complain."

"How's work?"

"Fine."

Christoph knew this was a blatant lie. Things were never fine in Michael's jobs. "Glad to hear it. Did you get the package I sent you? Did Paul like the book?"

"We've put it in the shelf for now until he's a bit older."

Christoph bit his lip. That was crazy. He'd sent a picture book! There was no minimum age requirement for the book. He stopped himself from saying what was on the tip of his tongue. "I thought I might drive down and see you one of these days," he said quietly.

Michael didn't take long to come up with excuses. "You know, we've got a lot going on at the moment. I'll be in touch when we've got more time." Christoph knew he'd be waiting till the cows came home. "I guess you're also pretty busy at the moment," his son added.

"What do you mean?"

"Isn't there some investigation going on?"

"How do you know about that?" He hadn't talked to Michael since shortly after his emergency landing.

"Come on, Christoph. There's something about the near-crash almost every day in the Blitz."

Christoph grimaced. Clearly his son still read that awful rag. "Don't believe everything you read in the tabloids. We did our best and we managed to get the plane back down to the ground."

"But a man died."

"That wasn't my fault." At least that was the opinion of the doctors. Apparently Mr. Prandtl had already suffered from a weak heart due to an infection, and all the excitement on board had simply been too much of a strain. The doctor hadn't stood a chance of resuscitating him.

"The way Mama's death also wasn't your fault?"

Christoph felt his pulse rising. How often would he still have to listen to this? "It was an accident!" He could feel his voice rising.

"You were driving!"

Yes, thought Christoph. He hadn't seen the damn van! Wasn't it enough that he blamed himself every single day? How long was this going to go on? "I'm telling you ..." Christoph stopped mid-sentence. There was no point. Every conversation with his son since Elena's death followed the same pattern, like an endlessly jumping record. It would be followed by a bitter exchange of words and then they would start shouting at each other and then Michael would simply hang up. There was no point. "Goodbye, Michael," he said quietly and ended the conversation.

He had always had a difficult relationship with his son's family. Elena had somehow managed to maintain a friendly connection. But ever since the fatal accident, the rift between them had become unbridgeable.

Christoph took the phone back to the sideboard and placed it back on the base station. Only now did he see there was a message on the antiquated answering machine. He pressed the button and played it back.

"This is Mrs. Prantl." He immediately recognized the voice. It had been etched into his memory during their conversation on the plane. "I would like to invite you to visit me at my home. Perhaps we can talk." This was followed by an address in Siegburg near Bonn. "Just come by when you have time. I'm almost always at home. Thank you."

Christoph took another bottle out of the fridge and slumped back down in the armchair. He had wanted to go the old man's funeral, but his lawyer and the legal advisor of his airline had advised him against it. He had wanted to write the woman a letter to express his condolences again, but he had been advised against doing that, too. Especially since he couldn't be given the blame following the medical report, it seemed shabby and downright rude to keep avoiding the woman. After all, he had been the pilot in charge. At least the airline had taken good care of the widow. Christoph had frequently checked that the woman was receiving the best possible assistance. He decided to accept her invitation. He wouldn't even ask his lawyer. And if they wanted to use it against him during the investigation or subsequent legal proceedings, well then by God, so be it.

5

Herbert laid a freshly picked bunch of wildflowers on the grave, right in front of the wooden cross that he had fashioned out of left-over pieces of wood from the workshop in the bunker. On it he had engraved only the name of his wife. No dates, no dedication. Apart from him, nobody else was likely to ever stand in front of this grave.

He adjusted the position of the flowers slightly and, tears in his eyes, gently stroked the rough surface of the cross. Then he stood up with difficulty and took a few steps back. The topsoil covering the grave rose up in a little heap, but with the next rainfall it would flatten out. In the end, a level area would be left, which would be overgrown with grass, like the other ten graves surrounding it.

Herbert closed his eyes and murmured a silent prayer. Over the course of the years, he hadn't lost his faith, despite the grimness of their existence. He refused to believe that in this hell, which they themselves had created on Earth, they couldn't hope for a better existence in the hereafter.

The gurgling of the nearby stream sounded unnaturally loud in the silence. Herbert opened his eyes and looked at the picturesque ruins of the old monastery, just visible between the trees. A few birds twittered in the trees. The atmosphere was peaceful, almost romantic. There were certainly worse places to be laid to rest. Herbert thought sadly that there would be nobody left to bury him when his time was up. It probably wouldn't be long now. He was feeling his age. And there was hardly anything left to eat in the bunker, despite the fact they had rationed the meager rests for weeks. It had taken all of Herbert's strength to dig the grave, place the body of his wife in the hole and fill it again. Now he was exhausted and drained.

Weakly, he shuffled through the abandoned grounds of the monastery, past the former guesthouse, the roof of which had caved in years ago, because there had been nobody to repair it. At the edge of the grounds, Herbert stepped out onto a road full of deep cracks and turned left toward the bunker. As he marched toward the tunnel entrance he mulled over how to keep going. Whatever happened, he had to start searching for food soon. For decades, the soil had been too contaminated to even think of eating any plants or animals, and their attempts in recent years to grow vegetables had all but failed. In summer and fall they had started to eat wild fruits and berries, and had even been able catch the occasional hare and rabbit. No doubt they were still contaminated, but it was better than starving to death. But Herbert was getting too old and weak to do much hunting, and with winter approaching he needed some basic supplies. He would take the last functioning jeep and scour through the ruins of the nearby villages for any remaining tins of food. But deep down, he knew it was pointless. Over the past few decades they had already found and taken anything that was left. No; this time, he would have to go further afield.

He laughed at the thought of it. There had been a time when he had refused to describe the dark, cold and musty bunker as home, but over the years they had gotten used to it. And in any case, there was no alternative. Their friends who had tried to live their lives outside the bunker were now all dead or had disappeared.

Herbert reached the heavy steel door that led into the mountainside. He stopped in front of it and turned around. The sun was high in the sky and gave off a wonderful warmth. The weather on this fall day was so pleasant, he would have loved to get a blanket and lie down on the wild grass next to the stream. But it wasn't wise to stay outside too long. Even now, so many years after the catastrophe, everything around here was still contaminated.

On the other hand, did it make any difference to him now? His life was slowly but surely drawing to a close, and there was nobody waiting for him in the bunker anymore.

Herbert shrugged and sat down in the grass next to the road. Just half an hour!

6

The taxi stopped in front of a seventies' bungalow in the Wolsdorf neighborhood of Siegburg. Unlike many comparable houses that Christoph had seen in Wiesbaden, this one was clearly well looked after. The bright white façade had recently been given a fresh coat of paint. Christoph paid the taxi driver and got out of the car. He had left his own car at the airport in Frankfurt. After a long day of hearings, he had walked to the station and taken the train to Siegburg. The train trip had taken only forty minutes.

A short, paved path led from the sidewalk to the front door. Christoph could hear the distant murmur of cars speeding down the nearby A3. He walked past a couple of carefully tended bushes in clay pots, and climbed a couple of narrow steps to the front door. There was no nameplate, but he checked the number again, and saw that it corresponded with the address Mrs. Prandtl had given him.

He stretched out his index finger and hesitated briefly before pressing the bell. He had no idea why Mrs. Prandtl wanted to talk to him, her voice on the answering machine had been neutral. It could be that she wanted to discuss the events on the plane with Christoph, but it was just as likely that she wanted to blame him again for her husband's death. But regardless of what her intentions were, he felt the need to talk with her and to tell her again how sorry he was. On the train he had already pondered over why it was so important to him. Was he hoping for forgiveness, so that he could absolve himself of his guilt? Or maybe talking to Mrs. Prandtl was a kind of substitute for a talk with his son after Elena's death.

Christoph remembered his lawyer's warning not to make contact with Mrs. Prandtl, but now he was here. He took a deep breath and pressed the bell. He heard a deep bong reverberate through house, and a few moments later he was looking into the surprised face of Mrs. Prandtl. Her expression softened and she smiled weakly before opening the door wider.

"I didn't expect you to come, Mr. Wilder." She gestured him inside. "Come in."

"Thank you." He stepped into a bright hallway. After Mrs. Prandtl had closed the door, he handed her the bunch of flowers he had bought in a little shop at Siegburg station. "Thank you very much for your invitation," he said, more stiffly than he had intended.

Mrs. Prandtl took the bunch of flowers, removed the paper and put them straight into in a vase, which seemed to be on the sideboard for just this purpose. This woman must have received many bunches of flowers in her life. "Thank you, they're lovely. They have very nice flowers at Katrin's Flower Shop."

"How did you know …?" The paper was neutral. He could have bought the flowers anywhere.

Mrs. Prandtl laughed. "My husband had friends and partners from all over the world who regularly visited us. Almost all of them who arrived by train in Siegburg bought flower's at Katrin's. Over time, you develop an eye for where they were bought. Come with me, we'll go into the dining room."

Christoph followed Mrs. Prandtl into a big, bright room. The floor was tiled in a pale gray. A large, expensive-looking wooden table with ten matching chairs dominated the center of the room. He imagined the Prandtl's had frequently hosted dinner parties. The sun fell through the floor-to-ceiling window, bathing the room in a soft light. An archway led into the adjoining living room.

"Please, have a seat. Coffee?"

Christoph nodded. "Yes, thank you."

Mrs. Prandtl disappeared through a doorway. Christoph lowered himself into a chair. He could hear the pumping and hissing of a capsule coffee machine and a short while later his hostess reappeared with a tray in her hands. She served Christoph and herself coffee in silver cups. Then she put milk and sugar and a plate of biscuits on the table.

"I did not expect to hear from you. I thought your lawyers would advise you against contacting me."

Christoph nodded. "They did."

"And still you decided to come and see me?"

"Yes, I have felt a need to talk to you all this time."

"Why, Mr. Wilder?"

Christoph hesitated. In his mind he could see his lawyer shaking his head. Every sign of openness, every honest word, could be used against him in court as an admission of guilt. But Christoph did not believe this was why she had invited him. No, he wouldn't act diplomatically. He was here to talk with the woman openly. "Because I feel responsible for your husband's death. I don't mean guilty! But responsible in the sense that on that night, I was responsible for the aircraft and its passengers. Despite all the problems, we did our best to land the plane and we succeeded. I don't think we could have done anything differently, or better. Nonetheless, your husband died on that flight. And I am sorry for that. You cannot imagine how sorry I feel. I just wanted to tell you that again."

The old woman looked him in the eyes and held his gaze for a long time. Then she nodded. "I know you did everything in your power to land the plane, and probably you and your colleague in the cockpit saved all the other passengers from death." She hesitated. "I invited you for a very particular reason. I want to apologize for what I said to you after we landed."

Christoph shook his head. "You don't have to—"

Mrs. Prandtl raised her hand insistently. "Yes I do. I passed judgment too quickly and blamed you for my husband's death. He would not have approved. It was wrong of me, and I think it is only fair to ask your forgiveness."

Christoph swallowed. The woman must be about eighty, and the deep lines in her face corresponded with her age. But the energy in her voice made Mrs. Prandtl appear decades younger. "I am not angry with you," he said quietly.

"I have had a lot of time to think in the last few weeks," Mrs. Prandtl continued. "And I have come to the conclusion that my husband's time was simply up." She stood up and walked over to a bookshelf in the living room. The uppermost shelf, which Mrs. Prandtl was just able to reach on tiptoe, was filled with photo albums. She pulled out a big, leather-bound album and returned with it to the table. With a look of concentration, she searched for a particular page and pushed the album across to Christoph.

All of the photos showed a man, in middle age, together with other people. "That's your husband," Christoph said.

Mrs. Prandtl didn't reply and continued to look at

the photos.

"Hang on, that's Henry Kissinger, the former US Secretary of State." Christoph' eyes fell on another photo. "And that's François Mitterrand, the—"

"The former French President, yes."

"What was your husband's job?"

"At the time my husband was a civil servant in the Ministry of Research and Technology in Bonn, and responsible for bilateral cooperation. He was often away with delegations and enjoyed his travels."

Christoph nodded understandingly. "You must have been alone a lot."

Mrs. Prandtl smiled. "No. My husband took me with him as often as he could. In those days it was still the done thing. Of course, I also often stayed at home alone, but we had a big circle of friends. It was a happy time in our lives. And when he retired fifteen years ago, we had many friends all over the world whom we visited and who visited us. On that last flight, we were on our way back from visiting Jim Bell."

"I'm afraid the name is unfamiliar to me."

"Jim was Minister of Agriculture a long time ago. We met up with him and his wife Christine in New York and went to the Met together. We saw Carmen."

Christoph wasn't sure how to respond. The Prandtl's had obviously led an illustrious life. He couldn't begin to imagine what it would be like to know politicians and dignitaries all over the world and to fly to America just to go to the opera. It couldn't be more different from his own life. Sure, he also traveled around the world for his job, but there was nothing very glamorous about it.

"In any case," Mrs. Prandtl continued, "my

husband enjoyed his life. He loved to travel, and I'm sure he would have preferred to die this way than to suffer a prolonged illness." She paused. "But that doesn't change the fact that I miss him and that the life I too enjoyed so much is over." As she spoke these last words, her voice, which had been so brisk up to that moment, cracked a little.

"Do you have children to take care of you?" Christoph asked quietly.

Mrs. Prandtl smiled weakly. "No, we never had any time for that. We toyed with the idea, but my husband rose up the ranks of the ministry in the early sixties, and we decided to put his career and the freedom to travel first. We decided not to have children. Can you understand that?"

As a pilot, Christoph was also often away, but there had always been long periods when he had been at home and closely involved in his son's upbringing. And Elena had never minded putting their son first. She had been happy in her role as housewife and mother. No, Christoph couldn't imagine not having children for the sake of traveling. But other people had other priorities. "That's a decision that everyone has to make for themselves."

"I'm glad you see it that way. We often met with hostility. But when we were younger, social norms were very different from what they are today."

"Where did you meet?" Christoph asked.

Mrs. Prandtl laughed again. "In kindergarten, you could almost say. We grew up almost as neighbors in Bad Godesberg. We were even born at almost exactly the same time. In 1939. After the war, our mothers didn't have much time for us, and most of the time we were outside playing in the rubble. Those memories had a strong influence on my husband. He was committed to making the world a more peaceful place; that was also what guided him through his career at the ministry. He believed that international cooperation in science and research was the way to show people that goals could be better achieved if we worked with each other and not against each other. In any case, from that point on we were inseparable. Later, I worked in a factory sewing blouses in order to finance my husband's degree in politics. But that is all a long time ago."

"Do you have friends who are there for you now?"

"Yes, we are part of a close-knit community here in Bonn. In terms of friends, and also financially, you don't need to worry about me." She paused. "But of course, friends who visit you regularly are not the same as a partner at your side."

"No, of course not," Christoph said, knowing only too well what she meant. "Listen, if there is anything I can do for you, please let me know."

She looked at him, but her gaze seemed to pass right through him. "I'm OK." Her eyes filled with tears. "But I have one wish that I know you can't fulfill for me."

"What is it, Mrs. Prandtl?"

The vacant expression on her face disappeared and she gave him a penetrating look. "Bring me back my husband!"

7

"You're early," said the blond secretary in a rasping voice undoubtedly caused by a high consumption of cigarettes. Her cool smile expressed disapproval. "Mr. Dickmann is still in a meeting. Take a seat and I'll call you."

Christoph shrugged, turned around, and left the anteroom. In front of the windows was a small group of brown leather chairs and a low glass table piled with copies of the latest issue of the airline's employee magazine. He filled a cup at the water dispenser, above which hung a photo of a 747 in flight, and looked down at the apron of Frankfurt Airport. A 777 was parked there, and mechanics were in the process of removing the engine cowling. In the distance, an A320 in the bright colors of an Eastern European airline was coming in to land.

Lost in thought, Christoph watched the hustle and bustle of the airport. He would miss it. …

He had thought it over for a long time. At first he had been happy that the investigation into the incident was over and that his conduct, as well as that of his first officer, had been praised as exemplary. This was corroborated in the final report. He had his pilot's license back and would be able to get back to flying. Perhaps on the same routes he had flown in the past and which he loved so much.

But in the days that followed he had got to thinking, as he sat around in his far-too-quiet house. The talk with Mrs. Prandtl had made a lasting impression on him. Her husband was dead, and although the report did not hold Christoph responsible in any way, it would never be the same as before. He came to the conclusion that it was time for a change of scene.

"Mr. Dickmann will see you now," Christoph heard the smoky voice of the secretary behind him. He emptied the plastic cup in one gulp, screwed it up in one hand and threw it in the garbage can next to the water dispenser. Then he followed the woman.

She opened a heavy wooden door and Christoph stepped into the office of his superior. Kurt Dickmann was a large man, and he heaved his rotund body out of the black leather chair with some difficulty before stretching out a large, fleshy hand. It was hard to believe that this corpulent man had himself been a pilot many years ago.

"Good to see you, Christoph."

"Thanks, Kurt. Good to see you, too." Christoph took the man's sweaty hand and shook it briefly. Then he sat down on the chair that his boss indicated. With a suppressed groan, Dickmann collapsed back into his chair.

The office was spacious and light. Large windows afforded a spectacular view of the Taunus mountain range. The tip of the Feldberg kept disappearing behind gray clouds that had been offloading drizzle over the airport all day. Although the view was wonderful, Christoph was sure Kurt would have preferred a view of the airport.

"I was delighted to hear the hearing went so well. I wanted to see you to discuss your future."

Christoph nodded. "Yes, there are a few things we should talk about."

The smile disappeared from Kurt's face and his expression became serious. "I'm glad you feel the same way."

Phillip P. Peterson

Christoph scrunched his brow in irritation. He thought his boss had just called him in to tell him he could resume his old flights.

"What do you mean?"

"I mean, we need to continue to keep you out of the firing line."

"Out of the firing line?" Christoph asked in confusion. "The investigation acquitted me of all responsibility and even praised us for our conduct."

Kurt nodded. "That's true, but unfortunately nobody will read it. The public is only interested in what it says in the papers."

"And what *does* it say in the papers?" Christoph tried to keep the irritation out of his voice.

"Nothing." Kurt paused dramatically. "That's precisely the problem. Shortly after the emergency landing, the papers were full of rumors and speculation. Particularly the things that singer said … What's she called again? Never mind. In any case, dirt sticks in the public eye. People will remember your name."

Christoph could feel his cheeks becoming flushed, but he stayed calm. "There is no dirt, Kurt. We did nothing wrong."

"You know it, I know it, and our colleagues know it—but the public doesn't and doesn't want to. Your name will be associated with this story for some time to come. Put yourself in the position of the supervisory body. Of course they want to prevent the headline 'Disaster pilot Wilder back in the air!' from appearing in tomorrow's *Blitz*."

Those damned tabloid journalists! They had no qualms about dragging a man through the mud—based on nothing more than rumors and speculation.

But if you were officially rehabilitated, it wasn't worth a printed apology or even a small report. You simply disappeared out of the spotlight and couldn't get rid of the dirt that was now stuck to you.

"Kurt, I wanted to change something in my life anyway. Send me to another airport, let me fly other routes. I'll gladly go back to short-haul flights."

Kurt shook his head. "You won't be flying any of our routes for the foreseeable future," he said quietly.

Christoph sat in shocked silence. He was being fired! The airline's image was more important to the managers than loyalty toward its own pilots.

No more passenger flights … His airline didn't have any freight flights. If he couldn't fly passenger aircraft anymore, what other options did he have?

"Do you really want to demote me to a desk job?"

Kurt raised his hands. "Honestly, we've thought long and hard about what we can do for you. First, we wanted to try and place you with another airline. Perhaps one in the Middle East, where nobody has ever heard of you, but that wasn't possible, either."

Christoph wouldn't have done that, in any case. To be stationed in Dubai or Bahrain? No, then he'd rather look for a new job himself.

"There are several office job options," Kurt continued. "Or we could do with another trainer in the simulator."

Christoph liked the simulators, but it wasn't the same as actually flying.

"I would prefer to fly."

"Then the only possibility would be to work as a flight attendant until the grass has grown over this story and management decides you can return to the cockpit. But it's possible that will never happen."

"Any other options?" Christoph asked.

"None," Kurt replied. "We don't have anything else to offer."

Christoph was stunned. He couldn't believe he would be prevented from flying. What else did he have? If he wanted to continue working as a pilot, he would have to look for another airline. On his own. And that would be difficult, especially if he wanted to maintain his standards. Sure, the low-cost airlines were always looking for pilots, but then he would have to accept a much lower salary. That was not a prospect he relished. Maybe he should take on the job of trainer in the simulator and try to get back in the cockpit when things had blown over? But how long would that take?

Kurt sat behind his desk and didn't say a word. He didn't give the impression that there was anything else to say.

Christoph shrugged helplessly. He needed some time to think about this new situation. He got up and brushed the creases out of his jacket. "Thanks, Kurt."

His superior got up, too. "I'm sorry, Christoph. It wasn't my decision. Think about which option you could envisage trying. No rush. After all, the last weeks haven't been easy for you." He accompanied Christoph to the door and opened it for him.

"The guy from the German Aerospace Center called again," the secretary rasped grumpily.

Kurt rolled his eyes and groaned. "I'd forgotten about him. I …"

Christoph was about to leave, but Kurt shot him a strange look. "Hang on, Christoph. Maybe I have something for you after all."

Christoph followed his boss back into his office.

Kurt leaned over his desk and began to rummage through a pile of papers. "Where was it? Where did I put that letter?" he muttered.

Christoph waited.

"Ah, here it is. I'd completely forgotten. The German Aerospace Center sent me a request a few weeks ago. I didn't have anyone and ignored it for the time being. They wanted to know if we had a pilot they could borrow. It's specifically aimed at someone with A380 type rating."

Christoph didn't know what to make of any of this. It sometimes happened that other airlines sent that kind of request if they were temporarily low on pilots. He knew the German Aerospace Center had aircraft and used them to test out new technologies, but usually they had their own, well-trained test pilots for that purpose. "What do they want, exactly?"

Kurt's eyes flew over the piece of paper, then he turned it over but the back was empty. "I don't know. It was phrased so vaguely that I decided to ignore it. It seems they've chartered an A380 for a scientific project and are looking for another pilot. It doesn't say anything else. In terms of what they're looking for, you would fit the bill. If you want, I can pass on your details. Oh yes, and it's based in Cologne-Bonn."

That was strange. Normally the German Aerospace Center carried out its test flights from Oberpfaffenhofen in Bavaria, where it had its own airfield. His only guess was that the nerds wanted to test out new instruments in flight. New navigation systems or something. Christoph knew he might just be flying in circles over the Rhineland, while the engineers and scientists sat at their computers and instruments in the cabin. It wasn't a very exciting prospect, and he wasn't surprised that Kurt had forgotten about the letter. A satisfied airline pilot would never get involved in something like that. But for Christoph, it would mean he could fly again. And Cologne-Bonn airport was near enough that he wouldn't have to move away from Wiesbaden. "What's the timeframe of the project?"

"No idea. Doesn't say. I need to call this Mr. Reuter. Shall I make an appointment for you?"

Well, it couldn't harm to check it out, at least.

"Sure, Kurt."

8

Christoph beeped his horn. The man on the sidewalk stopped as Christoph pressed the button to open the passenger-seat window. "Excuse me," he shouted. "Can you help me?"

The man was wearing threadbare jeans and an old, tattered windbreaker, the collar of a checked shirt peeping out at the neck. Christoph could tell at a glance that the guy was an engineer.

The man came up to the car and leaned down to look through the window. "Yes?"

"I'm looking for the Institute for ..." He looked down at the pass again. "... for Quantum Chronometry."

The man shrugged. "Never heard of it." Then he turned around and continued on his way as if he'd never stopped.

"Damn," Christoph cursed under his breath, and looked at the little map on the back of the pass, which had been given to him at the front gate after his ID card had been checked.

Following his talk with Kurt, Christoph had hung around at home for two days and waited. Then, finally, one of the management team had contacted him and told him he had an interview with a Mr. Reuter the following day at the German Aerospace Center in Cologne-Wahn. At midday he had set off by car and taken the A3 up to Cologne. There had been a traffic jam at Limburg, and after taking a detour through the Westerwald forest, he'd arrived at the grounds of the institute far too late. The complex was big, and he had difficulty deciphering the map. Or the guy at the gate had marked the location of the building in the wrong place. At the place indicated on the map there was a three-story house, but the big sign at the entrance read "Institute for Aerodynamics." Maybe the best thing would be to go back to the gatehouse and get the guy to explain the way to him again in more detail.

Christoph looked around. He wasn't even sure anymore in which direction the main entrance to the complex was. He sighed and steered the car into a lot that was empty apart from a few other vehicles. He turned off the motor, got out and went to the entrance of the building. Just before he reached the door, a man opened it from inside and smiled at him.

"Mr. Wilder?"

"Yes," Christoph answered in surprise.

The man was around fifty years old, tall, and had short dark-brown hair flecked with gray around the temples. "I'm Martin Reuter." He reached out a hand to Christoph.

Christoph shook it and pointed at the sign next to the door. "I thought you worked at the Institute for …"

"Quantum Chronometry. That's correct." Reuter said. "We only moved into the building two weeks ago, we're still waiting for a sign. I actually told Mr. Dickmann to warn you."

"I guess Kurt forgot …"

"Probably. In any case, I'm glad you made it. Come with me—we'll find an empty meeting room. My office is still a bit of building site."

Christoph followed Reuter into the building, which appeared to have been built in the seventies. The hallways were dark and narrow. The interior felt more like an old tax office than a modern research institute.

They walked upstairs to the first floor, Reuter taking the steps two at a time with his long legs. In the corridor on the first floor, a young member of staff wearing a yellow sweatshirt came toward them, staggering slightly under the weight of a big removal box. "Shall I take it down to the storeroom?" the man asked.

"No, that's Frank's. Just put it in his office," Reuter answered as he passed him by.

"My internet still isn't working," the man complained.

"Don't tell me. Call the IT guys," Reuter called after him. Grumbling, the young man disappeared into the stairwell.

Reuter opened a door and waved Christoph inside. Three beige plastic tables that had been pushed together in the center of the small room, and were surrounded by several chairs. A whiteboard on the wall was filled with formulas and curves jotted down in a scrawling hand. Several boxes of books were piled up in one of the corners.

"Coffee?" Reuter asked.

"No thanks, but I'll have a water."

Reuter indicated a chair and Christoph sat down, while his host opened a cupboard and took out a bottle of water and a glass, which he placed on the table. Then he sat down opposite Christoph.

"Did you have a good trip?"

"Unfortunately there was a traffic jam on the A3. My GPS wanted to take me another way, which unfortunately ended in a bit of an odyssey through the Westerwald. I'm sorry I'm so late."

Reuter smiled and made a dismissive gesture with

his hand. "Fits into the general chaos. Why should it be any different for you than for us?"

"You said you've only been here for two weeks. Where were you before?" Christoph asked.

"Our team worked in the Max Planck Institute of Quantum Optics in Garching. The team grew a lot in the last few years, and now we've been broken up. Because of the possible applications of our work, we got funding from the Ministry of the Interior and the Ministry of Defense and decided to enter into a collaboration with the Helmholz Society, of which the German Aerospace Center is also a member."

Christoph was not very familiar with Germany's research landscape. But he knew that politics played a role in the competition for research funding. "Why is the Ministry of the Interior interested in quantum research?"

Reuter laughed again. "Officially our work is about quantum cryptography. And encryption systems play a big role in home security these days. We've been given more than a billion euros by the Ministry of the Interior."

That seemed like a lot of money for a single project, but what did he know? But he was irritated by a word that Reuter had used. "What do you mean by *officially*?"

Reuter hesitated a moment as if considering how much he could tell Christoph about his project. "Our work is secret, as it has to do with aspects of national and international security. That applies in particular to the work affecting your possible position."

Christoph leaned back in his seat. "Listen, I'm a pilot. Normally I'm paid to fly an aircraft. I don't know anything about your area of research and haven't had anything to do with research work in general in the past. Just tell me what you need me for, and what you expect from me."

Reuter turned around and looked out of the window. "Behind that building the grounds of the German Aerospace Center come to an end. Beyond it is the Wahn Heath and Cologne-Bonn Airport, which is situated in a conservation area." Christoph spotted a small passenger aircraft taking off beyond the line of trees. "And the German Air Force base is there. In one of those hangars is an A380 which we have chartered and which represents the core of our work."

"What do you need an A380 for?"

"Do you know Sofia?"

"Yes, I've flown there quite often in the past, when I was still flying short-haul routes."

Reuter looked perplexed, then broke out into laughter. "I don't mean the city in Bulgaria." He needed a moment to compose himself, and brushed the tears of laughter from his face. "I mean the scientific project."

Christoph raised his hands. "Never heard of it."

"It's a joint project run by NASA and the DLR— the German Aerospace Center. A powerful telescope has been installed on board a Jumbo jet and is being used to observe the stars.

Christoph vaguely remembered hearing something once about a telescope on board an aircraft, but he wasn't sure if it had been in connection with this project. "But why put a telescope on an aircraft?"

"The biggest obstacle in astronomy is the blurriness caused by the atmosphere, which also filters out a large percentage of the light spectrum. On board an aircraft flying at an altitude of seven miles, you are above ninety percent of the atmosphere's volume of air and have a far better view of the stars."

"Makes sense," Christoph conceded. "And so you have a telescope on an A380?"

Reuter shook his head. "No, not quite. We've set up a different scientific experiment on the aircraft."

"Not a telescope …"

"No."

"What then?"

"I'm afraid I can't say." Reuter paused briefly. "It's really hot stuff. You'll be amazed when you take on the job. So?"

"So what?"

"Are you on board?"

This was going too fast for Christoph. "Hold on. I need a bit more information. For one thing, I'd like to know what the pay is."

Reuter nodded. "Sure. You will keep your contract with your airline. We could employ you directly, but then we could only pay you a salary in line with the civil service pay scale. By buying you in, so to speak, we can ensure an adequate salary."

"Good. For how long do you want me?"

"Our project will run for five years, to start with. We would employ you for that period."

"And if I want to leave sooner?"

"Of course you will have the usual notice period. That's up to you. But once you find out what it's all about, you won't want to leave. I promise."

The scientist was clearly very excited about his project. But Christoph was sure this experiment—or whatever it was—wouldn't impress him that much. He might not even understand what it was about.

Ultimately, it didn't matter anyway. He would play the flying bus driver for the scientists and engineers—nothing more. "Where will we fly to?"

"All flights start in Cologne and are limited to German airspace. With the exception of an area over the North Sea, which will be closed to normal air traffic during our test flights."

"Don't you have your own test pilots?" Christoph asked.

Reuter smiled. "Yes, we do. But they've finished their work on the aircraft. Your job is not to carry out test flights but simply to fly the plane. Meanwhile, the experiments will take place in the cabin."

Christoph nodded. It was as he had feared: he was going to be the chauffeur! He ran a hand through his thick hair. Should he accept the offer? Flights only in German airspace? Boring. If he had had a choice between his old scheduled flights and this job, it wouldn't have taken him long to decide. But in his current situation he didn't have much choice, unless he wanted to be stuck in the simulator.

Shit! He was stuck between a rock and a hard place.

"OK, I'm interested."

Reuter clapped his hands exuberantly. "Great! Welcome on board!" He stood up and reached out a hand to Christoph.

Christoph took it in surprise. "That fast? Don't you have any other applicants?"

Reuter laughed again. "No. We sent our request to several airlines. But you're the only one to apply. Which surprised me."

Christoph wasn't surprised.

"And time is of the essence, we want to get started

next week. We have two of our own pilots, but one of them has health issues and the aviation medical examiner declared him unfit to fly. Everything has been prepared and we can't wait any longer. I presume you are able to start right away?"

"Yes, I have no more commitments in Frankfurt."

"Good. Then I can work out your duty roster tomorrow."

"Can you tell me anything more about the job, now that I've agreed to do it?"

Reuter shook his head. "Not yet. We still need to run a security check on you. I'm going to request that it's given top priority—everything should be ready tomorrow."

"So we'll see each other tomorrow?"

Reuter nodded. "Yes. And I have a suggestion: Why don't you spend the night in Cologne-Wahn. I'll book a nice hotel for you at our expense, and you can come straight to the aircraft on the military air base tomorrow morning at six. I'll make sure they have a pass ready for you at the gate."

Christoph took a moment to consider. He had nothing to do at home and he always traveled with an emergency overnight bag in his car. "Sure."

"Wonderful. I would invite you to dinner this evening, but unfortunately I have another appointment in Hardthöhe, at the Ministry of Defense. But we'll do it another day."

"That'd be nice."

"So I'll see you tomorrow," Reuter said. "And Christoph …"

"Yes?"

Reuter laughed mischievously. "Get ready to be amazed!"

9

"Very discreet paintwork," Christoph said to Martin Reuter.

He had entered the hangar through a side door. At the entrance to the Cologne-Wahn airbase he had been given two passes, but it was only possible to enter the hangar with a magnetic card. After ringing the bell several times, a man in blue overalls had finally opened the door and taken him to Reuter, who was working in a small meeting room. Christoph had greeted his new boss warmly and together they had gone into the hangar, which was just big enough for the Airbus A380. The plane was bright white, as if it had been freshly painted. There was no writing on the fuselage, and no logo on the tail.

"Well, the project is top secret. There are already photos of the plane circulating on the internet, taken by plane spotters, but they think we're testing out new avionics."

"Do you have my security clearance?"

"Yes, it arrived half an hour ago by fax."

"So now you can tell me what these flights are all about."

Reuter nodded and smiled. "Of course. Allow me to keep you in the dark just a little longer. Maybe you can guess. Let's board the plane." He set off toward the A380.

As they walked around the aircraft, Christoph noticed that, like on a freight plane, there were no windows in the fuselage apart from a small area on the lower deck behind the cockpit. They reached the mobile stairs and Christoph followed Reuter up the steps. The door to the aircraft was open and a few seconds later they were standing on the lower deck.

Christoph looked around in bewilderment. It looked so different from the passenger cabins he was used to. Right next to Christoph were three rows of four seats. The rest of the cabin was filled with computer consoles. This aircraft—which normally held five hundred passengers—couldn't transport more than twenty people. At the moment, Christoph and Reuter appeared to be the only people on board. The steps that usually led up to the upper deck weren't there at all.

"Is this it?" Christoph asked.

"Yup, this is it. This is where the scientists carry out the experiment during the flight."

"What experiment?"

Reuter seemed either not to have heard the question or not to want to answer it at the moment. "The rest of the aircraft contains the technical equipment for our experiment as well as lots of analysis and monitoring devices, which can be operated from these consoles."

Christoph shook his head. "You mean you've crammed the whole plane full of scientific instruments?"

"Yes, and although this is one of the biggest aircraft in the world, it was quite a struggle to reduce the apparatus to an amount we could fit on board. Come with me, we'll go to the cockpit. Werner is waiting for us there."

"Werner?" Christoph asked.

"Your first officer." Reuter opened the door into a narrow corridor that connected the cabin with the cockpit. As they walked along it, Christoph noticed that the flight crew rest compartment had been removed. There was a door in the middle of the corridor, but behind it was just a storage room lined with several shelves and a small galley, which had been moved from the cabin to the front of the plane.

Reuter knocked on the cockpit door and opened it without waiting for an answer. "Hi Werner."

Christoph followed him into the cockpit. A thickset man of medium height, wearing blue overalls, was sitting on the pilot seat, a checklist in his left hand, a ballpoint pen in the other. Werner turned around. His grin revealed gleaming white teeth of a shade that could only be achieved by bleaching. Or they were false. "Hi Martin." He fixed his gaze on Christoph. "You're Wilder?"

Christoph stepped forward and proffered Werner his hand.

Werner put down his checklist and pen and returned the handshake. "Werner Linde. Welcome on board."

"Thank you, it's good to join the team."

"I've heard all about you."

Christoph shrugged. "I've been in the news a few times recently."

"Yeah, I followed the investigation. It wasn't always fairly reported in the media."

"No," Christoph answered.

"I presume that's why you're here now."

"Yes, I can't fly for my airline for the time being."

Werner grinned at him. "Doesn't matter. This is ten times better, right?"

"Is it?" Christoph replied.

"He doesn't know yet," Reuter replied.

Werner bellowed with laughter. "Well, get ready for the surprise of your life!"

All the secrecy was starting to get on Christoph's nerves. "Can't you stop beating around the bush? What have you got back there?"

Reuter nodded. "The whole upper deck is taken up by a linac."

"A linear particle accelerator?" Christoph asked in confusion. "Why?"

"Let me explain," Reuter said. "As I said, we are affiliated with the Institute of Quantum Optics."

"Yes, you told me."

"Together with a working group, I carried out research on photon entanglement."

"Entanglement?" Christoph felt out of his depth. The scientist would have to explain it to him a little more simply.

"Yes, you can connect particles quantum-mechanically. The particles then share certain properties. If you study particle A, then you immediately know the value of particle B, even if it is light years away."

Christoph didn't really understand what he was talking about and shrugged. "And why is that important?"

"It means that information can be transmitted instantaneously. It contradicts the relativity theory, which claims that nothing can move faster than light. Not even information."

Christoph had to admit it sounded impressive, but what did it have to do with the A380? "Continue."

"We've discovered that a wormhole forms between the two particles. The information is transmitted through it."

"A wormhole? But that's science fiction!" Christoph responded in disbelief.

Reuter laughed. "You ain't heard nothing yet! We connected two particles and got one of them up to almost the speed of light with an accelerator. Einstein's theory of relativity claims that time dilates at such high speeds. Do you realize what we have achieved in this simple but astonishing way?"

Christoph shook his head but he had an inkling.

"We sent one end of the wormhole into the future. By repeating the process again and again, we can venture as far as we want into the future. With the help of a virtual, cosmic string, we can also travel to the past."

This was crazy! "Are you trying to say you can send particles through time?"

Reuter nodded. "And more. We've managed to enlarge the originally microscopic wormhole using vacuum energy."

Christoph still didn't quite understand. So these nerds could create a big wormhole and—incredible as it sounded—generate a portal to the past or the future. If it was true, it was beyond belief.

The whole situation was unreal. Christoph expected the moderator of *Candid Camera* to step into the cockpit at any moment. But instinctively, he knew that Reuter wasn't lying. The decisive question was why they had to carry out these experiments in an aircraft. It didn't make sense. Unless ... Christoph suddenly felt his heart racing and his hands trembling. No, it was impossible!

Werner Linde grinned at him. "He's got it! I almost passed out myself at the time," he said, looking at Reuter. "Yup, Wilder. We're gonna travel through time with this aircraft."

10

"Welcome to our meeting," Reuter announced. He was standing behind a table and tapped away on his laptop as he spoke his introductory words. They were sitting in a room on the second floor of the hangar. Christoph, and a few others who had also just joined the project, were about to be filled in on the details. But Reuter started with some general remarks and projected an organigram of the institute onto the wall. Christoph found it difficult to concentrate on what he was saying.

It was crazy. Completely crazy! Christoph still couldn't believe what Reuter and Linde had told him on board the A380. A time machine in an airplane!

In fact: that machine in the cabin turned the Airbus *itself* into a time machine. He would no longer be the pilot of a jet, but the pilot of a time machine!

"Mr. Wilder, please stand up and introduce yourself."

Christoph, sitting in the front row, flinched as he heard Reuter say his name. He stood up abruptly and turned around so that the others in the room could see him. There were around twenty other people in the room. Most of them were wearing blue overalls with the DLR logo—two overlapping black rhombuses on a white background. The team was made up almost entirely of men, of all ages. He could see only two women.

He introduced himself and briefly outlined his career to date. He didn't mention the incident over the Atlantic. Instead he explained how, after completing his aviation training, he had started his career with a regional airline in Munich, before changing to his current airline, where he had started to fly long-haul flights and completed his A380 type rating training. "I look forward to being involved in this interesting project and to working with you as a team." He sat back down in his seat.

"Nice speech." Werner Linde whispered in his ear.

"Thanks."

"Thank you," Reuter said from the podium and nodded at Christoph. "We also look forward to working with you. I'm sure you will get to know the members of our team quickly. I would also like to introduce Max Jung and Franka Weber."

A young woman waved cheerfully, and a younger man with blond hair sitting next to her gave a brief nod.

"Franka is a physicist," Reuter continued, "and will be involved in the theoretical side of the project. Max is an aircraft mechanic and has transferred here from another DLR institute." He cleared his throat. "For those of you who are new today, I would like to briefly outline the background of the project."

Reuter began by explaining how the project had been called to life in his old institute, before moving on to a tedious lecture about particle collisions and the entanglement of photons. Christoph didn't understand much of what Reuter was saying and found himself scanning the room. The other members of the team, who had been part of the project for longer, appeared to be bored. A chubby man around forty had closed his eyes and was taking a nap. Two younger men whispered and kept glancing over at the new physicist. With her fine features and long brown hair, she had clearly already distracted some of her male colleagues. A gray-haired man was playing around with his cell phone.

Finally Reuter moved on to more interesting things, and Christoph turned his attention back to the podium. "Next week we want to start on the first experiments. Together with the ministries involved, we have developed a preliminary plan." He stooped down and rummaged in his black leather bag. Finally he pulled out a binder and laid it in front of him on the lectern. "Our first objective is to determine the physical parameters of time travel. What is the exact diameter of the wormhole we've created? How long does it remain stable? Does the amount of energy required correspond with our theoretical prognoses?"

"Excuse me," Christoph heard a woman's voice from the back. He turned his head and saw that the new physicist had raised her hand.

"Yes?"

"How much energy do you think will be required, and what are you using as your energy source?"

Reuter nodded. "Good question. We expect an output of around one Gigawatt for two seconds. The energy will come from one of two high-performance capacitors, which will be charged on the ground. So we can do one trip into the past or future and back per flight. Interestingly, it is irrelevant how far forward or back we go. Whether it's one second or ten years doesn't make any difference to the amount of energy consumed."

Christoph raised his hand. "But is there a limit to how far we can travel into the past or the future?"

"Theoretically the possibilities are limitless, but practically speaking, no more than about eighty years."

"Practically speaking?" Christoph prodded.

"Every leap into the past or future involves some spatial displacement, which is beyond our control. That's also why we installed the time machine in an aircraft. We will carry out the leap in time at an altitude of three miles. The further we distance ourselves from the present, the greater the spatial displacement. For eighty years the displacement is about three miles. If we move too far away from the present, we risk coming out in the Earth's interior core, which wouldn't be healthy for the aircraft or its occupants."

A man behind Christoph chuckled.

"We can also travel further from the present, but then we would need a space ship and would have to carry out our experiments in space." Reuter grinned. "If we're successful, this might be exactly what we end up doing. Imagine an observation satellite that can travel far into the past. We could watch Jesus at work, or view the dinosaurs from orbit. I am confident this will happen one day." He cleared his throat. "We are the pioneers. The first time travelers. We will make history."

"Quite literally," Werner muttered.

Christoph felt uneasy. If Reuter had really found a way of traveling through time, there must be risks involved. This was all going too fast for Christoph. He thought about all those science-fiction films, in which time travelers went back in time and changed history with terrible consequences ... what was the word?

Christoph stood up. "Aren't you afraid of a ... what's it called ... a time paradox?"

Reuter smiled. "We have taken that into account. In fact, the purpose of our first trips will to investigate precisely these dangers. Don't worry. I'll get to that in a minute."

Christoph sat back down.

"Mr. Wilder has a valid point, but of course it is nothing new to us. In our first series of tests our aim is no more and no less than to investigate the nature of time." Reuter pressed a key on his laptop and a map of Germany appeared on the wall.

Christoph could see a line that led from Cologne up to the North Sea. It was probably supposed to indicate the flight route.

"We will depart next Tuesday evening. We will fly up to an exclusion zone that has been specially reserved for us over the North Sea, and from there we will make the first journey through time ever to be undertaken by mankind."

A man behind Christoph clapped. "Finally!"

Reuter continued. "We will travel back exactly twenty-four hours, fly a big curve, take some measurements and return to the present. Less than fifteen minutes later."

"On Tuesday …" the new physicist mused aloud. "Then surely we would see the aircraft on the radar screens on Monday morning? We could watch ourselves on our trip into the past before we even set off."

Reuter shook his head. "No, that's precisely what we *won't* do. We have requested for our exclusion zone not to be monitored by radar. We have a tracking station, but we won't analyze the data before we get back on Tuesday.

"I see," Ms. Weber interjected. "But what if we can observe ourselves and then decide not to go on the flight? Then we would have a time paradox."

Reuter grinned. "Yes, we will in fact deliberately create time paradoxes in one of the later flights. Very small ones of course, in order to look at how time works, and to analyze the consequences."

Christoph shook his head. If he was sitting in the cockpit on Tuesday and returned to Monday, then theoretically he would be able to speak to himself over the aircraft's radio. "This is madness!" he whispered to Werner Linde, who simply raised his eyebrows in response. Christoph couldn't shake off the feeling that this project was playing with the very foundations of their universe. And he wondered if it was really such a good idea to have become involved.

"We are scientists. Since we have developed this technology, it is our duty to use it for scientific purposes." Reuter smiled and his eyes shone brightly. "Maybe we'll even find an answer to the fundamental questions of human existence. Where do we come from? Where are we going?"

11

"To be honest, I don't like any of this," Christoph said, sipping at his glass of beer.

"Why not?" Werner asked.

The meeting had lasted all morning. Then Christoph had returned to the A380 with Werner and they had sat in the cockpit discussing the features of the aircraft. Due to the machines in the back part of the cabin, the aircraft was relatively heavy, and needed more fuel than an equivalent passenger plane. This reduced its range, but since they weren't going to be using the modified A380 for intercontinental flights, it didn't really matter. What's more, the cockpit—which was usually designed for two pilots—had room for an extra workspace. It was situated behind the pilot seats, where in older aircraft the flight engineer would have sat. It was from here that the time machine was monitored and run, although the engineer—Reuter, for the initial flights—would be assisted by his colleagues at the consoles in the cabin.

At the end of a long day, Christoph and Werner had gone to a nearby restaurant to get to know each other better. Christoph was sure he would get on well with the cheerful and affable Werner. But he couldn't shake off the feeling that the time-travel technology was riddled with risks.

"I can't stop thinking about time paradoxes. Personally I think the past is the past and should stay that way," Christoph said.

Werner shrugged. "Martin said that for now, they're only interested in testing the methodology. In fact, part of what we're doing is finding out if time travel poses a risk or not."

"Yes, but what if we find out that the technology *is* dangerous? Would Reuter then destroy his machine?"

Werner opened his mouth to answer, but Christoph wasn't finished. "And even if he did: the technology is no longer secret, and even if we were able to keep it secret, it would only be a matter of time until other teams, other nations, worked it out. If you ask me, Pandora's Box has been opened and nobody is going to be able to close it again."

Werner smiled. "I think you're being too negative. It gives us an opportunity to iron out our mistakes, and to find out more about the past. Imagine being able to actually see Jesus! Wouldn't that be incredible?"

Christoph gazed into his beer glass. "And if we don't like what we see?"

"Then we'll have to deal with it. What counts is the truth. Think of the crimes we can solve … or perhaps even prevent."

"Crimes?" Christoph asked.

Werner nodded. "It will be one of our most important missions. That's why the Ministry of the Interior is involved in our project. The A380 has already been equipped with sensors. After a murder, we could simply fly back a few hours into the past and film the crime with our cameras. We could deal with planned attacks and send in special forces to arrest the perpetrators before they ignite the bomb."

"Which brings us back to time paradoxes," Christoph retorted sharply.

Werner laughed. "I can't imagine that such a thing exists. It's just a theoretical construct. We change the past and have a new present. That's it."

Christoph shook his head slowly. "I don't think it's

that simple."

"Well, we'll find out soon enough," Werner said. "Next Tuesday, in fact. Until then it's all just speculation."

They sat in silence for a moment. Christoph picked up his beer glass and swayed it gently back and forth.

"I heard that your wife died," Werner said quietly.

"Yes, a year ago," Christoph answered.

"What happened? Was she ill?"

Christoph shook his head slowly. "No, a car crash. We'd rented a convertible for the weekend and spent a night at a hotel in Monschau in the Eifel." Christoph took a gulp of beer. He didn't mention that Elena hadn't really liked going on their little jaunts anymore. "On the way home, a van pulled out in front of us. It all happened so quickly. Suddenly we were lying upside down in a ditch. I unbuckled myself and crawled out of the wreckage. I didn't even have a scratch. But on the passenger-seat side the A-pillar broke. Elena broke her neck and died immediately.

"I'm sorry."

"Yeah, me too." Christoph took another gulp of beer.

"Imagine you could save your wife and avoid the accident," Werner said tentatively.

Christoph almost coughed up his drink, banged his glass back down on the table and shouted: "My wife is dead! And nothing will bring her back to life."

"But—"

"No," Christoph said. "I don't want to talk about it anymore."

And yet … the idea hadn't even occurred to Christoph since finding out about the time machine that morning. Undoubtedly, he would have thought of it himself at some point. Was it really possible? Might they be able to go back and prevent the accident? But that was another time paradox. On the other hand, it would be easy enough to try. Or he could go back, and bring Elena back with him to the present. Then it wouldn't be an accident, but a kidnapping. You could twist it so that he thought his wife was dead at the time, and thereby avoid a paradox. But he would still be changing the past. It was enough to drive you crazy just thinking about it.

Christoph pushed the idea aside. The whole experiment would probably be a gigantic flop, and they would find out that it was impossible to change the past. He had never been very religious, but he doubted that God or the universe would allow that kind of meddling.

"I'm sorry," Werner said.

"It's OK. Let's change the subject," Christoph suggested. "How about you? Any family?"

"No, I'm a dyed-in-the-wool bachelor. You can lead a fuller life."

"Well, I guess everyone has their own view on that. A girlfriend?"

Werner grinned. "At the moment, two."

"Two?" Christoph spluttered. "I take it they don't know about each other?"

"Sure they do. It's more fun as a threesome!"

Christoph wasn't sure he wanted to hear any more details. "Where are you from originally?"

"I was born here in Cologne—grew up here and stayed. I love the mindset of the people and I love the city. I can't imagine living anywhere else."

Christoph had never cared where he lived. He had

moved so often that he only associated the word *home* with wherever he happened to be living. If he stayed involved in this project for a longer period of time he would probably move to Cologne. It's true he would be even further away from his grandson then, but since Michael and Andrea hardly ever let him visit, the extra ninety miles wouldn't make much difference. "Did you fly for a commercial airline in the past?"

"No, never." Werner laughed. "I trained as an aircraft mechanic with the DLR. At the same time I trained as a pilot at Bonn-Hangelar, after I'd already gotten my glider pilot license. The DLR paid for my commercial pilot license and type rating training. For a while, I was a flight instructor for the European Astronaut Centre in Cologne."

"And how'd you get involved in this project?"

Werner emptied his glass in a single gulp. "I love Kölsch, but the glasses are just too small." He paused. "Well, I was involved in the project from the start as a consultant, and applied for the job of pilot when it came up. I did my type rating training in Frankfurt; unfortunately I didn't have enough flight hours to be made captain. But first officer isn't bad, either."

"You had another captain before," Christoph suddenly remembered.

Werner nodded. "Freddy, yeah. He was thrilled to get the job. Then he had a routine check with the aviation doctor. And that was that."

"The aviation doctors …" Christoph said darkly. He never had a good feeling when he went for his routine checkups. You went in with your pilot's license, but nobody could say if you would come back out with it. And your health only ever went downhill, never up. "What was the problem?"

"Abnormalities in the ECG. Erratic heartbeat—which isn't uncommon. But for a pilot, it's a no-go."

"And what is …" Christoph began.

"Freddy."

"Right, Freddy. What's he doing now?"

Werner shrugged. "Had himself transferred to Oberpfaffenhofen. Scheduling test flights—back-office work." He looked at his watch. "Shall we get the bill? Tomorrow's going to be a long day."

"Yes," Christoph agreed and waved over the waitress who happened to be looking in their direction. He fished his wallet out of his jeans' pocket. "I'll get this."

"Thanks."

12

Herbert loaded the last box onto the jeep. He pushed it right up to the others and then climbed down from the truck bed. He stretched and groaned loudly. The hours of packing and loading had taken their toll on his back.

He picked up the clipboard and made sure he hadn't forgotten anything on his list, then he walked around the jeep, and pulled the tarpaulin over the truck bed, securing it with string. At this time of year, it could rain at any time.

He had toyed with the idea of spending the winter in the bunker and only setting off the following spring, but the prospect of months alone in the cold, gray bunker under the mountain was unbearable. Even at the best of times, he had found it hard to think of the bunker as home, but since his wife had died, the rooms had lost any shred of homeliness they might have once had. What if, one day soon, he simply didn't wake up again one morning? After all, he was now at an age where this was perfectly possible. Then the bunker would become his final resting place—and Herbert simply couldn't bear that idea.

No, he wanted to head south and see what he found along the way. Not that he had any illusions. He would probably never reach a place of safety. He consoled himself with the thought that it was about the journey, not the destination, but he also knew that all that awaited him at the end of his journey was death.

Herbert shrugged. He had made up his mind and would rather meet his end out here than slowly waste away down in the bunker.

He took one of the canisters from next to the workbench, unscrewed the gas cap and poured in the fuel. With the gas in the tank and in the canisters at the back of the jeep he would be able to drive several hundred miles. With a bit of luck he would be able to find more gas, enough to get him as far as the Mediterranean.

After screwing the gas cap shut, he left the garage, which was connected to the bunker's storage room by a big sliding door. He switched off the light and went straight to the living quarters, and to the tiny room where he had his bed. He had moved in here several days ago, and avoided going back into the room where Erika had died.

He opened the closet and took out a few more clothes that he wanted to wear the following day on the road. He drank some water from the glass bottle that stood on a table next to the bed. He wouldn't be having any supper, as he had eaten the last tin of potato soup, which was already long past its sell-by date, for lunch. When he set off the next day, the very first thing he would have to do was find something to eat. He already had a destination in mind, and he hoped that it hadn't been completely plundered since his last visit a few years ago. Otherwise his end really was near.

13

"OK, we've reached the target area. Let's start with the checklist," Reuter said. He was sitting behind Christoph and Werner at the flight-engineer console, which housed the time-travel controls.

"No, not yet," Christoph said. "We have to fly a little further north. The weather conditions are better there." They were now about sixty miles north-west of Helgoland. This marked the boundary to the test area. During the briefing, Christoph had also checked that they had the right NOTAMS. They were in a thick blanket of cloud, but according to the weather report, there was less cloud cover further north.

"We don't need perfect weather," Reuter said, irritably. "We'll do the test here."

Christoph turned around. The usually so affable project manager was barely recognizable this morning. He seemed nervous and agitated. Today's test was supposed to be a dress rehearsal for the trip back in time two days from now.

Christoph shook his head. "I would prefer if we had a good view of the sea in case there are any problems with the instruments during the test. We'll stay on course."

"I said we will do the test here! I am heading this project. I decide!"

Christoph was surprised. He hadn't expected such dictatorial behavior from Reuter. It was time to get a few things straight. "Mr. Reuter, I do not dispute that you are head of the scientific project. And in that capacity, you are responsible for carrying out the test as well as for the scientific instruments on board." He paused for a moment and looked Reuter straight in the eyes. "But I am the captain of this aircraft and responsible for its safety and the safety of its passengers. Which is why the decision about whether, when, and where the test is carried out is mine and the first officer's." Christoph saw Werner raise his eyebrows. He got the impression they had kowtowed to the project manager in the past, even if that wasn't standard practice in aviation. "When I give the OK, you can start to carry out the test. But I am in charge of the aircraft until we land."

Reuter was taken aback. He probably wasn't used to being talked to in this way. "I am in charge here!" he said, in an almost whiny tone of voice.

"Yes, you're my boss, Mr. Reuter. But that doesn't change anything about standard aviation practices, which are implemented for good reason. Too many plane crashes have been caused by unnecessary altercations between pilots and passengers."

"I am not a passenger!" Reuter's face was turning red. His thin upper lip quivered and he struggled to speak. He looked as if he were about to lunge forward and tear Christoph out of his seat in order to take over the controls. But that was hardly possible. "Alright," he said in subdued tone of voice. "But don't think this is the end of the matter."

"Of course, we need to sort this out as soon as we're back on the ground." This incident was sure to have repercussions. But tasks and responsibilities on board needed to be clearly defined.

They continued to fly northward in silence. Finally, they emerged out of the dense clouds and Christoph could see the surface of the water four miles below them. He checked the navigation display to make sure the outer boundary of the exclusion zone was far enough behind them, then he turned around and nodded to Reuter. Reuter looked at Christoph through narrowed eyes as if he wanted to stab him. He opened his mouth to say something, but closed it again. Then he pressed a button on his console that connected him to his team in the cabin via the intercom system. "We're starting the checklist for the test. Everyone at the ready." Reuter picked up his clipboard from the table in front of him and fished a pen out of his jacket pocket.

"Status of the aircraft," he said loudly.

It was Werner's job to answer this.

"Flight level sixteen thousand feet. Speed three hundred knots. Course three hundred and forty degrees."

Reuter jotted down the numbers. "IGS reset."

Werner flipped a switch on the center console. The IGS was an additional instrument guidance system. It was necessary so that they wouldn't be reliant on satellite and radio navigation on flights into the past.

"Collider?"

"Collider ready," a male voice crackled over the intercom.

"Capacitor?"

"Capacitor banks are charged und ready for operation. Bank number one active."

"Good. Casimir oscillator deactivated."

The Casimir oscillator was the centerpiece of the time-travel experiment. Christoph had understood that, at least, even if he hadn't grasped the physics. The wormhole was produced by the accelerator and the energy from the capacitor banks. The oscillator then somehow generated a "false vacuum", as Reuter had explained, which enabled the microscopic wormhole to be increased in size to such an extent that it surrounded the entire aircraft. It was this last step that they were testing out on today's flight. The first real journey through time would take place two days later.

"Oscillator is deactivated."

"Transponder out."

Christoph reached for the center console and switched off the device. He didn't have a good feeling. The transponder showed the position of the aircraft on the radars of the air traffic controllers and other aircraft. Now their A380 would disappear from those screens. But Christoph could also understand that those in charge of this time-travel project wanted to keep it top secret.

"Transponder is out," he said, which was acknowledged by Reuter with a quiet grunt.

"Aircraft prepared for time travel?"

Christoph re-checked all the instruments and made sure the autopilot was activated. Werner did the same. They nodded to each other and Christoph turned round to Reuter. "Aircraft ready for time travel."

Reuter looked at his console, on which all of the status displays were glowing bright green, apart from one. "I am activating time travel. In five, four, three …" His hands approached a big red button. "Two, one, now." He pushed the button down in one deft movement. Immediately, an ear-piercing alarm signal sounded through the cockpit. Christoph had expected it.

"That's because of the deactivated oscillator," Reuter explained. "Everything else seems to have worked. Bank one is empty, injector and collider have been released. The detector at the front of the vacuum tube registered the collapse of the wormhole."

"Collapse?" Christoph asked, reaching for the center console and switching the transponder back on.

"Yes, if it isn't inflated and stabilized by the oscillator, it collapses right away," Reuter replied and clapped his hands together. "Otherwise, everything went as planned. We still have to analyze the data when we're back in Cologne, but I would say we're ready for the big day."

14

"Hey Captain," Franka said as Christoph entered the cabin. She was sitting with two colleagues at a computer console.

"Good morning, Ms. Weber," he replied cheerfully. He hadn't seen her since the test flight.

The physicist waved him over. "Come and have a look."

Christoph had actually wanted to go straight into the cockpit to exchange some manuals that had been updated in the past few days, but he was happy to accept the pretty young physicist's invitation. "What's up?"

"Well, Captain, we're all on first-name terms here. Apart from Reuter, of course. How about it?"

Christoph had already noticed that the atmosphere in the research facility was more relaxed than at his airline, where many of his colleagues maintained a deliberate distance. But Christoph liked the relaxed atmosphere at the institute. And he also liked the team members he had met so far. "Thanks. I'm Christoph." He held out his hand to Franka.

A look of amusement crossed her face, then she stepped forward and to his surprise gave him a quick hug. "That's the way we do it where I come from." She grinned at him, revealing two gorgeous dimples. A strand of long, brown hair fell into her face. Even the blue overalls, which were a little too big for her, did not succeed in hiding her feminine curves. Over the past few days, it hadn't escaped Christoph's notice that she attracted more than the occasional glance from the male members of the team.

"You settled in quickly," Christoph said.

"Yup," Franka replied cheerfully. "It's a great team working on an even greater project."

"I'm Stefan." A burly man holding a screwdriver in his right hand leaned forward.

"Nice to meet you, Stefan. Do I need to hug you, too?"

Stefan grinned. "Nah, I'll let you off the hook."

"Glad to hear it." Christoph turned to look at the third person in the group, a lanky young man who always looked a little shy. "And you are?"

"Sende."

Franka giggled.

Christoph looked at the man in confusion. "That's not your real first name is it?"

Sende blushed. "No, that's what they call me. Comes from my surname."

"Which is?" Christoph asked.

"Sendenhorst."

Christoph nodded. "Like the town near Münster. And your first name?"

Franka was still giggling. Sende looked around helplessly.

"C'mon, tell him your first name, Sende," Stefan said with a grin.

"Horst."

"Horst Sendenhorst." Christoph suppressed a smile. "I see. OK, Sende. Nice to meet you."

"Thanks, nice to meet you too, Christoph."

"I've got a question," Stefan said.

"Sure."

"Do you also have a nickname? I mean something like 'Maverick' or 'Ace', like in *Top Gun*?"

Christoph chuckled. "No, usually only fighter pilots have nicknames. At my airline we addressed each other by our first names, so Christopher, or just Christoph."

"Christopher?" Franka asked.

"That's my real name. My father was American. He named me after his father, who died shortly before I was born."

"Are you an American? Cool," Sende said.

Christoph shook his head. "My mother was German. I'm both. I have dual citizenship."

"Where'd you grow up? In the USA or Germany?"

"I was born in New York, but I spent my early years in Germany. When I was five, we moved back for a few years, but then we came back to Germany for good."

"So do you see yourself more as an American or as a German?" Stefan asked.

"Both the same," Christoph replied. "I have relatives and friends in both countries, and I feel comfortable here and there. Even though I've been living in Germany for over twenty years now, mainly because I now have my own family here." He hesitated. "At least I had one," he added on a sudden impulse.

His comment was followed by an embarrassed silence. Sende looked at the ground. Stefan scratched his head awkwardly.

It was Franka who broke the silence. "Werner told me what happened to your wife. I'm very sorry."

"Me too," said Christoph, his voice sounding more bitter than he intended it to. "Anyway. What's done is done."

"Do you have children?" Franka asked.

"Yes, but unfortunately we don't get along very well. Let's change the subject. What are you working on here? Is there a problem?"

"No, not really," Stefan said. "We're just ironing out a few minor bugs that showed up on the test flight yesterday. No big deal. We need to recalibrate a few sensors that were indicating slightly different values. We'll take them out and bring them over to the avionics workshop.

"So—ready for the big day tomorrow?" Christoph asked.

Franka nodded. "Yup, we're ready. We can hardly wait."

"We'll be the first time travelers in history," Stefan said enthusiastically. "It's like being part of the Apollo crew during the first trip to the moon."

Christoph shrugged. "Apart from the fact that, unlike Apollo 11, our flight isn't being televised. In fact, it's shrouded in secrecy."

"At some point it'll be made public," Stefan grinned. "I'm already looking forward to the press conference. It's going to be crazy!"

"I don't think—" Christoph was interrupted by his work cell phone buzzing. He took it out of his pocket and answered. "Hello?"

It was Reuter's secretary. She told him he should come to the institute, where his boss was waiting for him. He would have to swap the manuals in the cockpit later. Christoph ended the conversation and turned back to the three young team members. "I won't hold you up any longer. We'll see each other tomorrow at the latest."

Franka and Stefan waved goodbye, Sende just nodded.

15

"Come in. Sit down." Reuter's voice was devoid of emotion. He was sitting at his huge desk, stony-faced. Clearly he hadn't forgotten about their argument in the cockpit. What a contrast to the friendly welcome he had received a week ago!

But Christoph had expected this. Calmly he sat down on the uncomfortable chair in front of Reuter's desk.

"Don't you ever dare to humiliate me again the way you did yesterday, Mr. Wilder."

Christoph smiled weakly. "I didn't mean to humiliate you. I simply informed you of my decision to start the test only once we had better visibility in the area assigned to us."

Reuter gave him a penetrating stare. His eyes narrowed to slits. "*Your* decision? *I* decide when we start the tests.

Christoph nodded slowly. "Yes, you decide when to start the tests. But only when you have the go-ahead from me."

"When I have the go-ahead from *you*?" Reuter repeated in a shrill voice.

"That's right," Christoph said.

"I am the head of this project!"

"The pilots, in this case Werner and I, are responsible for the safety of the aircraft, its crew and its passengers. We have the ultimate power of decision on board." Christoph spoke slowly and clearly. He felt like he was talking to a stubborn child. He knew his words weren't going down well with Reuter. Christoph thought it was important to be able to compromise and to foster a good working atmosphere, but he wasn't willing to go against his principles as a pilot.

"In the past, when Frederick Schröder was still our pilot, things looked different around here. I'm seriously wondering if I shouldn't hire another pilot."

He was threatening to fire him. But Christoph remained unfazed and didn't respond. "I don't know how you did things in the past, but there are clear regulations stipulated by the Federal Aviation Office, which are based on ICAO regulations. You can look them up online any time, which I recommend you do, so we don't have any further misunderstandings. I never met my predecessor and was unaware that you made decisions in the cockpit in the past, but I will be abiding by the regulations. Nothing more, nothing less. If you can't live with that, I recommend you start looking for my replacement."

Reuter stared at him angrily. He opened his mouth to say something, but shut it again immediately. Christoph was sure that Reuter knew perfectly well that he had no authority in the cockpit. Of course he could replace Christoph, but that would take a while, and it was unlikely that he would be prepared to postpone the first time-travel expedition. Christoph had no idea to whom Reuter was accountable. Probably some secretaries of state in the ministries financing the project. It certainly wouldn't look good if he fired a pilot because he complied with international regulations.

Christoph was surprised by Reuter's behavior. On the ground, he had always been friendly and collegial. He had only turned into a dictator when they were in the air. Was it because of the pressure or could there be a personal reason behind it?

"Alright, Mr. Wilder," Reuter said finally. "I will forget about it for the moment. Nonetheless, I think it's a great shame that the incident yesterday has thrown such a dark shadow over our working relationship. And just a week into your job. A great shame."

What was that all about? Was Reuter trying to give him a guilty conscience? "A good working relationship is very important to me, Mr. Reuter. I really want to maintain a positive atmosphere in the team. But my absolute top priority is the safety of the plane and its passengers. I am not willing to make any compromises there."

Reuter grunted quietly. "We'll see," he muttered.

"Is that all?" Christoph asked.

"No," Reuter said. "I have another assignment for you." He leaned forward, picked up two heavy files from his desk and held them out to Christoph.

He took them in confusion. "What is this?"

"This is your record of the test flight and that of the cabin crew. I would like you to consolidate both into one report. Since you are the pilot in charge, I thought it was your job."

Christoph tried not to let his anger show. Normally this was done by a secretary or a technical assistant, and he only needed to sign the finished report. He knew this was just a form of bullying—revenge for the altercation during the flight yesterday. It would take him hours to write the report.

"Do you have a problem with that?" Reuter asked.

If he refused, he would give Reuter a real reason to give him a warning. Christoph smiled weakly. "No. Of course not. When do you need it by?"

Reuter leaned back in his chair and smiled coldly.

"Monday morning will do," he said patronizingly. "That gives you the whole weekend to work on it."

16

"Happy birthday, Michael."

From the startled expression on his face, Christoph knew his son hadn't expected to see him here. But Christoph had known that if he called and asked to come by, Michael would have come up with an excuse: that they were out or had made other plans; something. Christoph had also known that his son would probably try and get rid of him even once he was standing on his doorstep. But nonetheless, he had got into his car and driven the long distance from Cologne to Heidelberg. Despite the fact that it was the day before the big test. Or perhaps for that very reason?

The truth was, Christoph had a queasy feeling in his stomach about the next day. They would be attempting something that had never been done before in the history of mankind. Something that had worked without a hitch in laboratory tests might end in a disaster tomorrow on board the plane. Although he seemed to be the only member of the team to entertain any doubts, he couldn't help thinking it was a risky business and wanted to at least see his family beforehand. Or rather, what remained of his family.

Michael had overcome his surprise. "What are you doing here?" he asked with a stony expression.

"I had something to do in the area," Christoph lied. He nervously adjusted his tie. "I just wanted to swing by and congratulate you on your birthday."

"You just wanted—" Michael murmured. From inside the house came the sound of laughter. Michael was probably having a party.

"Can I come in?" Christoph asked quietly. "I

won't stay long."

His son sighed, and the corners of his mouth turned down slightly. Once again, Christoph was painfully aware that he wasn't welcome here. But Michael shrugged and stepped aside. "Sure," he said flatly.

Christoph stepped into the narrow hall and waited until Michael had shut the door, then he handed his son a bottle. He had bought a scotch in a deli near his hotel in Cologne. He had chosen a very good one— the price had been exorbitant. Michael probably thought that Christoph was trying to make up for something—and he wouldn't be wrong. But no present in the world would make up for what he had done to his son.

Michael took the bottle without a word and placed it on the sideboard without giving it a second glance. "We have visitors. I won't have any time to talk to you. There are some drinks and food in the kitchen. You can help yourself." Michael turned around and walked into the living-dining area, where he walked up to a slim man in a light-blue jacket and appeared to pick up where he had left off in their conversation.

Christoph stood in the doorway feeling a little lost. He looked around: The terraced house that Michael and Andrea had rented was barely big enough for a family of three. But Christoph knew that rents in Heidelberg were high and that a large percentage of their income probably went toward living here. There were about a dozen people of Michael's age in the room. Andrea was sitting with several other women at the dining room table, a glass of red wine in her hand. She had looked up at him briefly when he came in and quickly averted her gaze. Just like Michael, who had immersed himself in conversation with the man in the blue jacket.

Christoph ran his fingers through his hair. His gaze wandered across the room and he considered which group he might be able to join, but he knew he would be out of place with any of them. Finally, he went through the little doorway into the narrow kitchen. Several bowls of salad and plates of appetizers were lined up on the worktop. Some frankfurters were being kept warm in a pot of hot water.

Christoph sighed and took a plate. He filled it with some pasta salad and fished a frankfurter out of the pot with some tongs. Then he returned to the living room, but hovered near the doorway to the kitchen.

As he ate, he asked himself where Paul was. Maybe his grandson was in his room playing.

A blond woman squeezed past him into the kitchen with a forced smile. Christoph gave a friendly nod and followed her. The woman looked around the kitchen before grabbing a bottle of ketchup.

"Nice party," Christoph said, trying to sound relaxed but knowing how stupid he sounded.

"Yes. You seem to be having a great time," the woman answered sarcastically.

"I'm Christoph," he said. "I'm— "

"I know who you are," the woman responded, still smiling rigidly. "Excuse me." She pushed past him and returned to the table where Andrea was sitting.

Christoph placed his half-empty plate next to the sink. He wasn't hungry any more. The best thing would probably be to leave. He wasn't wanted here. But before he went, he wanted to speak with his son.

He walked purposefully toward the bar table

where Michael was still talking to the man in the blue jacket. He stopped laughing abruptly as Christoph approached.

"I'll be on my way."

"Sure," Michael said coolly.

Christoph pointed toward the front door. "Can I grab you for a minute?"

Michael looked at him wordlessly and turned to his friend. "I'll be back in a sec, Christian."

"No rush," the man replied. "I'm going to get another beer from the fridge."

"Bring me one too," Michael said over his shoulder as he led his father into the hallway. He closed the door to the living room behind them. "What is it?"

"Where's Paul? I haven't seen him anywhere."

Michael sighed. "What time it is?"

Christoph cursed to himself. Of course, it was already nine o'clock. Paul was in bed asleep. Why hadn't he thought of that?

"Can …" Christoph swallowed. "Can I see him?"

Michael stared at his father without saying a word. Then he turned his head toward the living room door, as it to make sure it was closed. "Andrea wouldn't like it. Paul … Oh, what the hell, come on. But quietly!"

Christoph followed his son, who was padding quietly up the stairs. One of the steps creaked as Christoph stepped on it, causing his son to turn round at him and scowl. Upstairs, Michael switched on the light. Two doors led into two small bedrooms. The right one was open a crack. Michael peeked inside and then opened the door. Christoph stepped inside.

The light from the hallway fell onto a wooden cot.

Paul was lying on his stomach, but had his head turned to the side. Tufts of short, blonde hair stood up in every direction.

Christoph smiled. His grandson! He looked so peaceful, happy even. Still completely innocent, untouched by the trials and tribulations, the guilt and worries, that shaped the lives of adults. What path would this little man take in the future?

Christoph thought uneasily about the experiment he would be involved in tomorrow. He imagined traveling sixty years into the future. He could find his grandson and ask him directly what he had done with his life. Tomorrow, Christoph could discover what he would otherwise never know, since he would be dead in sixty years' time. And what if his grandson's path led to ruin? Would Christoph be able to change anything, or was the path of every human being in the universe predetermined?

Michael tugged at his sleeve and nodded toward the door. Wistfully, Christoph looked at his grandson one last time. If only he could have taken him in his arms just once! Sadly, he followed Michael down the hall and back downstairs to the front door.

"Thanks," Christoph said, as he buttoned his jacket. "That meant a lot to me."

"Please call next time before you come by," Michael said. "Andrea will give me an earful that I let you in at all."

"I'm sorry. I didn't want to cause any trouble." Christoph took a deep breath. "Listen, Michael. I know I've messed up. That my behavior toward you and Andrea wasn't always—"

"And Mom!" Michael interrupted.

Of course he had to bring that up again! Christoph

could feel his pulse quickening. "I am not to blame for Mom's death."

"There we go again. The old song and dance," his son retorted. "The other guy was to blame because you had right of way." He reached out his hand and thrust a finger at Christoph's chest. "I don't care what was said in court. You are also to blame. You and your dumb outings into the countryside with the convertible! And you always drive too fast!"

"I stuck to the speed limit!" Christoph protested.

"Just because it's legal to drive sixty miles an hour doesn't mean you should! If you'd driven slower or kept your dumb ass at home, Mom would still be alive."

"If I could undo what happened, I would!"

"But you can't undo it. Mom is dead! I have to live with it and so do you. But you could at least admit that you are responsible!"

Christoph' felt himself clenching his fists. "I am not to blame for the accident, for God's sake!" His voice grew louder. "Why do you want me to admit something that simply isn't true? The other—"

"Ssshh!" Michael hissed. But it was too late. Paul had woken up and was crying.

Michael opened the door. "Go!"

"I didn't mean to ..."

"Just go!" Michael hissed.

Christoph heard the front door slam behind him. He had messed up. Again.

17

"This is a great day in the history of mankind," Reuter said histrionically. "Perhaps even the greatest day in the whole of history."

The project leader was standing on the bottom step of the gangway. Christoph and the other members of the institute had been about to board the A380 when Reuter had begun his speech, as Christoph had guessed he would. Behind them, in front of the hangars, a row of luxury government limousines waited. Rolf Hasenbeck, the Minister of the Interior, was watching the proceedings with some other men in suits and generals in blue uniforms. Because the project was secret, they weren't having an official event. Nevertheless, Reuter had assigned a research assistant the job of recording the proceedings on video camera. Helmut knelt in front of the gangway and filmed Reuter from below, presumably to make the aircraft behind him look more impressive. Christoph suppressed a yawn and turned back to look at Reuter, who had spread his arms wide. His eyes were gleaming.

"Up to now it has been said that we live in the space age or the information age. But from today, we will be able to say that we live in the age of time travel. Until now, historians have had to rely on old stories, rumors, and ruins buried for centuries or millennia. Once we have completed our research program and equipped the first satellites—or even manned space shuttles—with our technology, humanity will be able to experience the past first-hand. We will be able to watch the pyramids being built; see how humans spread across the Earth. But we won't just revolutionize archaeology and anthropology. What we are doing today will have a huge impact on all areas of life. Take biology, for example. At some point, we will send off teams to witness the extinction of the dinosaurs. We will see Earth before the first organisms formed. Geologists will be able to study the emergence of the Mediterranean or observe historical volcanic eruptions. Physicists will be able to witness the moment in which our sun ignited and record it for all to see. And perhaps—yes, perhaps, one day—fearless explorers will set out to document the genesis of the universe." Reuter paused.

The people around him listened spellbound to his words. But Christoph felt uneasy. Secretly he hoped the test today would fail and that the project would prove to be infeasible. On the other hand, the night before, he had imagined again and again what it would be like to go back a year and rescue Elena. Or go back even further and prevent the falling out with Michael and Andrea. Would it really be possible? And if so, at what price?

"Today we will make the start," Reuter continued. "We will travel twenty-four hours back in time. We will prove that time travel is possible. When the veil of secrecy is lifted in a few months or years from now, we will be celebrated as heroes and our names will enter the annals of history."

Reuter is probably most concerned about his own name, Christoph thought. He looked around. His colleagues were still gazing at Reuter and hanging onto his every word. The suits were staying discreetly in the background, otherwise there wasn't much happening on the apron of the airfield.

If history was to be written at this moment, and time travel really was about to become possible, shouldn't there be tourists and researchers from the future present to attend this historic event?

Christoph shook himself and rejected this thought. You could go crazy if you thought about the consequences for too long!

"Let's go!" Reuter shouted ecstatically, raising a fist to the sky. "Let's write history!"

Franka clapped enthusiastically. Werner smiled. Others nodded in agreement.

Reuter climbed up the steps to the aircraft. Christoph and the others followed him.

"Everyone knows what they have to do," Reuter said. "Let's not lose any time."

The team of scientists, technicians, and engineers went to their consoles in the cabin. Christoph could hear fans starting up, and a constant beeping indicated that the computers and other instruments were being switched on. After making sure the aircraft door was properly closed, he followed Werner and Reuter into the cockpit.

He closed the door behind him, sat down in the captain's seat and pulled the seat forward a little. Werner had already activated the systems and had the checklist for starting the engines up on screen. Christoph checked that the flight plan was correct, since the briefing at the air base had been very cursory. The weather was perfect: a cloudless sky over the whole of central Europe would give them excellent visibility. Looking out of the cockpit windows, Christoph could see a picturesque, orange sunset. When they reached the test area, it would already be dark.

Christoph and Werner went through the checklist together.

"Fuel quantities as calculated. Calculations in the flight management system complete," said the first officer. Werner, who was usually so relaxed, seemed nervous, but Christoph put it down to the upcoming flight. He himself tried not to think about what lay ahead of them. He was the pilot and concentrated on his tasks. He didn't want to be distracted by any extraneous thoughts.

"Good, ready for engine start. Mr. Reuter!" Christoph turned around in his seat. "We're ready."

His boss turned away from his console and looked him in the eyes. "Your *passengers* and cargo are ready."

Christoph nodded, ignoring the sarcastic tone of Reuter's voice, and turned back to his instruments.

"One more thing, Mr. Wilder." Reuter's eyes narrowed. "Enjoy the flight. It will be the only time-traveling you do. I have already requested a replacement for you. Before the next flight, you will return to your airline in Frankfurt and can start your office duties there."

Christoph gasped. He knew Reuter was resentful, and wouldn't easily forget their confrontation two days ago, but he hadn't expected to be fired just like that. Surely Reuter must realize there were rules that needed to be adhered to when flying, and that it was in everybody's interest to stick to them. But apparently his pride couldn't take such a knock.

Christoph turned to Werner, who was staring at the instruments with exaggerated concentration, pretending he hadn't heard anything. Christoph took a deep breath and turned back to Reuter, who was smiling triumphantly and waiting for a response.

Well then, so be it. Better to work in the simulator than with a project leader who put his ego above flight safety. "I understand."

"Good. Then let's start!" Reuter said, leaning over his console again.

Christoph turned to Werner. "Let's continue with the checklist. APU start."

"APU start," Werner confirmed and switched on the auxiliary power unit above his head.

Christoph checked the set frequency and made radio contact with the air traffic controller. "Cologne Delivery, XF39."

The answer came right away. "XF39, Cologne Delivery."

Christoph confirmed that he had listened to the latest version of the ATIS information system and requested clearance to start for the test area over the North Sea.

"XF39, Information Echo is correct, cleared X-11 as filed, SONEB THREE UNIFORM, Squawk 1522, QNH 1012, XF39."

Christoph repeated the exact wording so that the controller could confirm he had understood the instructions correctly.

"XF39, Readback correct, Contact Cologne Ground, 121.72 for startup and pushback," said the controller.

Pushback was unnecessary, as they were already on the apron.

Christoph change the frequency and got authorization to start the four engines. Werner pressed the necessary switches. Christoph watched the RPM of the turbines rise and stabilize. "XF39, request taxi."

"XF39, taxi to holding point A1 runway 32R via B and A."

There was a light wind from the west. Christoph had expected the controller to send them to runway 32R, which meant they would have to roll the aircraft across the entire airport first. It would have been more practical if they could have used runway 06, which was right in front of them, but the A380 was too heavy for it.

Sighing, Christoph confirmed the instruction. He pushed the thrust lever forward a little and released the parking brake. Slowly, they rolled past the hangars of the military section of the airport. When he looked out of the left window, he could still see the ministry officials and the generals watching the plane's departure.

After a few minutes they passed Terminal 1, where several Eurowings and budget-airline aircraft were docked at the star-shaped satellite. It was now shortly after six in the evening and many aircraft were being prepared for departure. It would only quiet down again after eight, when freight aircraft dominated the night shift. Christoph steered the heavy aircraft onto taxiway A, which took them past the cargo area to the runway. Nobody spoke in the cockpit. Even the otherwise talkative Reuter was fully focused on his console.

Finally, they reached the eastern-most point of the airport. Following the instructions of the controller, Christoph stopped at the start of the nearly two-and-a-half-mile-long runway, which had been an emergency landing field for the space shuttle back in the eighties, which NASA had fortunately never had to use.

Christoph took a deep breath and looked to the west. Directly in front of him, the sky was streaked golden and red, and he could already see a few stars glinting in the sky.

Finally, the controller gave them clearance for takeoff.

"Runway 32R, cleared for takeoff, XF39," Christoph confirmed. "OK, all clear?"

"All clear," Werner replied.

"Then let's go," Christoph said and pushed the thrust lever all the way forward.

Slowly at first, then faster and faster, the heavy aircraft roared down the runway.

"One hundred knots," Christoph said.

"One hundred and fifty knots, rotate," Werner said.

Christoph gently pulled on the sidestick and the nose tilted upward. A few seconds later they were in the air.

"Gear up!" Christoph instructed his first officer.

Werner pulled the landing gear lever up and confirmed: "Gear up."

Shortly after taking off, Christoph changed course to 015, in order to follow the assigned route. Once they had ascended a few thousand feet, the voice of air traffic controller came in over the loudspeaker: "XF39, contact Langen Radar, 118.75, have a good flight."

Christoph changed the frequency and activated the autopilot. Gradually, the aircraft rose to a height of fifteen thousand feet.

"You have control!" Christoph said to Werner.

"I have control," the first officer confirmed.

Christoph turned around to Reuter. "We'll reach

the test area in about twenty-five minutes. Weather conditions are good, so we can start at the southern end."

"Good," Reuter replied curtly.

Christoph cleared his throat. "Is it really necessary to replace me? After all, I'm just doing my job and sticking to the ICAO regulations."

Reuter stared back at him without a hint of emotion. "I am of the opinion that you do not fit into the team. I'm sorry. It's nothing personal."

Nothing personal?

"Perhaps we could—"

"What? Talk about it?" Reuter interrupted him sharply. "I have made my decision. Now please excuse me, I have to carry out a thorough system check so that we can launch the test program on time."

Christoph sighed and turned back to the controls. A few minutes later, the Airbus had reached today's cruising altitude of twenty thousand feet. Christoph looked out of the window and could see the lights of Münster below. Werner was informed by the air traffic controller that he had passed on control to his colleagues at Bremen Radar, in whose area they were now flying.

Before long they had reached the coast and shortly after that the test area over the North Sea. Christoph felt a knot in his stomach.

Traveling through time!

They would travel back twenty-four hours. To yesterday! Even if they deactivated the transponder, they should already be visible on the recordings of the radar screens from the day before.

"Reuter!"

"What is it?" Reuter sounded annoyed.

"Did you check yesterday's radar records?"

"No," Reuter replied. "I explained it to you already. We have saved the records and have them under lock and key. We will only look at them after our trip, to see if they match the log books of our aircraft."

"But we could have learned something from them. What if we had looked at the records but didn't find a trace of our aircraft? That would mean we failed."

Reuter shook his head. "Not necessarily. We know too little about the nature of time to draw reliable conclusions from preliminary results. That's precisely why we're doing these test flights. "We—"

"We are now flying over Emsland." The first officer wasn't speaking to them but on the interphone to the cabin crew. "I repeat, we are now flying over Emsland."

What was that all about? Why would the physicists and technicians care about the area they were flying over? "Why—?" Christoph began, but Werner shook his head. Christoph looked at him in confusion.

"Wait and see," Werner said. He was stony-faced, and his tone had lost all its usual cheerfulness.

"Werner! What's going on?"

The first officer reached under the seat, pulled out a pistol and pointed it at Christoph.

"Werner!" Reuter had become aware of what was going on. "What are you doing?"

Werner pointed the pistol at Christoph with his right hand, while he pushed back his seat with his left. He got up and stood behind Reuter. "Get up!"

"Werner! Goddammit, what the hell—?"

"I said, get up!"

Reuter took off his headset and put it on the console, without taking his eyes off Werner. Slowly he got up.

"Sit on the first officer's seat."

Reluctantly Reuter sat down next to Christoph. "What are you doing?"

"A little change to the program. We have a new destination," Werner replied drily.

A hijacking? Christoph shook his head incredulously. But why? Was he planning to share the time-machine technology with another country? It didn't make any sense. Christoph looked at the transponder. If he managed to change the code to 7500, they would know on the ground that something was wrong.

"Don't even think about it," Werner said coolly.

Of course; Werner was a pilot. He knew the tricks and wasn't going to be screwed over. But Christoph still couldn't believe that his first officer wanted to hijack the aircraft. "Which course should I take?" he asked.

"Continue to our test area over the North Sea."

"But you just said you wanted to go somewhere else, so where—"

"Not where; when!"

Reuter let out a muffled cry. "Werner! You don't seriously want to—"

"We want to," Werner said loudly. "And we will!"

"We?" Christoph asked.

"I'm not alone. My partner is in the cabin and keeping the cabin crew in check."

Partner? What the hell was going on here? Was Werner part of some kind of organization? Christoph felt like he was in a bad secret-agent thriller from the sixties.

The buzzer on the door sounded.

"Open it!" Werner said.

Reluctantly, Christoph flipped the switch which unlocked the cockpit door. In came ... Max!

The young technician who had joined the team a week ago together with Christoph was also carrying a weapon. There were beads of sweat on his forehead.

"Everything OK out back?" Werner asked.

"Yup, all under control! Fresh from the computer," Max said huskily and handed his accomplice a black USB stick.

"Good. You can return to the cabin and check that nobody sabotages the equipment. We'll reach the test area in ..." Werner studied the navigation screen, "... ten minutes. Then we'll get started."

The young man turned around and disappeared back into the cabin.

"Werner! You can't change the programming of the time machine. You can't—"

Werner held the USB stick under Reuter's nose. "I can! The grid is fresh from the simulator." He stepped backward until he was standing at Reuter's console and inserted the stick into a USB port. Werner lowered the pistol toward the floor as he fumbled with the keyboard and trackball.

If Christoph acted fast, maybe he could grab the weapon. Should he ...? No, it was too risky. If Werner fired the pistol here in the cockpit, it could mean the end of everyone on board.

"Werner, listen to me!" Reuter gasped. "The time machine is completely untested. Please don't tell me you want to travel into the future, or further into the past than twenty-four hours! We don't know if it's safe. You need to know that—"

Werner silenced his boss with a wave of the hand. "We're going to go back further in time than twenty-four hours," he said. "Much further."

Christoph felt his stomach churn. "Where do you want to take us?"

Werner finished whatever he was doing at the control console. He glanced up at Christoph and Reuter and twisted his mouth into a smile. "The new course is set. Our destination is November 7, 1939."

Was he serious? He must be out of his mind!

"You're mad," Reuter whispered. He had turned white as a sheet. "That's it, you must have gone mad!"

Werner grunted. "I've never been more sane in my life."

"We can't go back to 1939! That's almost a hundred years!" Reuter's voice was rising in panic. "We don't know the exact spatial variance. We might come out under the earth or in space!"

Werner gave a dismissive wave. "I've done the math. Two miles variance over a hundred years. No problem."

"That's just in *theory*!" Reuter cried.

Werner laughed out loud. "Suddenly you don't trust your own calculations? That's a change!"

"What do you want to do in 1939?" Christoph asked quietly.

"Prevent one of the biggest catastrophes of mankind."

1939 was the year the Second World War broke out. He must mean that. "How do you plan to prevent the war? That's impossible!"

"We will eliminate the man responsible for it," Werner said drily.

"Hitler!" Christoph whispered.

Werner nodded. "You got it." His tone was resolute. "We will kill Adolf Hitler!"

18

"You're crazy! Totally crazy!" Reuter screamed. His face was bright red.

"It's our chance to prevent the greatest crime in human history."

"Werner!" Christoph said urgently. "It won't work. What are you thinking? That you can kill Hitler and then travel back to a present in which the Holocaust and the Second World War never happened?"

"We won't find out if we don't try," Werner said obstinately.

"Aren't you afraid of a time paradox?" Christoph asked.

"I don't believe such a thing exists. We'll change the past and that's it."

"I'll take you to court, Werner! You can't get away with this!" Reuter roared.

"Sit down and calm down," Werner said, raising his pistol threateningly.

"I'm telling you, I'll—"

Christoph winced as Werner hit Reuter on the head with the butt of the weapon. Reuter sank back in the seat, whimpering. Blood ran down his cheek and accumulated in a red spot on the collar of his shirt.

"We're already over the North Sea," Werner said, glancing at the screens. "Switch off the transponder and radio!"

Christoph raised his hands defensively. Werner's plan was crazy. Completely crazy. He needed to stop it. Somehow. "Think about what you're doing! We have no idea if the time machine even works. I—"

Werner's right hand jerked forward to the center console. With a few deft movements he had switched off the radio.

"Change course to zero-ten, altitude sixteen thousand feet!"

"Werner, I beg you ..." Christoph was surprised by the imploring tone of his own voice.

"Get a move on! Or do I have to do it myself?"

Christoph sighed and adjusted the autopilot, and the aircraft began to climb. Werner stood in front of the controls of the time machine. He picked up the headset, which was lying on the console and pressed the speaker button. "Max, do you hear me?"

Max's reply came right away. "Yes, I hear you."

"Everything under control back there?"

"Yes, they're doing exactly as I say."

"Good. I need a green light from all stations."

"Coming right up."

A few seconds passed, the status indicators on the console changed one after another from yellow to green.

"Are we in the test area?" Werner asked.

Christoph didn't answer. He was still feverishly considering what he could do. Would Werner really go as far as to use his weapon? Christoph remembered his fateful flight over the Atlantic a few weeks ago. What if he just switched off the engines and made sure they couldn't be started again? Of course they would have to make an emergency landing, but he would manage that somehow. Hamburg and Bremen weren't far away. On the other hand, they weren't flying very high. It would be incredibly risky. But better than having this madman play around with history. All he needed to do was reach up and switch on the fire extinguisher system in all engines.

Christoph could feel his hand twitching.

But Werner sensed something. He pointed his weapon straight at him. "Don't do anything stupid. I swear I'll shoot you if you get in my way!"

Christoph raised his hands. It was pointless.

"I asked if we are in the test area yet!"

Christoph nodded in resignation.

"Max, we're ready to go. If you're still standing, you should probably sit down and buckle up," Werner spoke calmly into the interphone. Then he sat down in Reuter's seat, still holding his pistol, and got to work on the console. "The grid for the oscillator was accepted," he said triumphantly. One by one, he flipped several switches and muttered to himself: "Capacitor, injector, valves to open. Oscillator active. That's it."

Werner smiled at Christoph. "We will make the world a better place."

"Or destroy it," Christoph said loudly, but Werner did not respond.

"I will activate in five, four, three—"

"Don't do it!" Reuter whimpered.

"Two, one, now!" Werner punched the red button with his fist.

19

A loud humming noise sounded through the cockpit, but quickly became quieter and abruptly stopped. The aircraft vibrated slightly, as if it had entered slight turbulence, but this subsided after a few seconds. Otherwise nothing happened. They flew on through the night over the North Sea.

"Strange," Werner said. "Nothing happened. Did it work?"

Christoph looked at the navigation screen. They were apparently still flying through the test area. Then his eyes fell on the altimeter. "Hey," he said. "We've lost some height. We're flying at fifteen thousand four hundred feet. The autopilot switched to the new altitude." They had also lost the GPS signal and radio navigation. At least the inertial navigation was working.

Christoph looked out of the window. A moment ago, illuminated by the light of the moon, they had been able to see the surface of the North Sea. Now there was only darkness below them. The moon ... A moment ago he had been able to see the half moon setting in the west. Now it was ... gone?

He turned in his seat and glared at Reuter. "Congratulations. Your time machine seems to have worked."

Reuter stared at him open-mouthed. His face and shirt were dotted with dried clots of blood. "You mean—"

Christoph nodded. "The moon is gone. So we're not in the present anymore."

Reuter's gaze wandered from Christoph to Werner, who was grinning triumphantly. "It worked!"

Reuter whispered. "But where are we exactly?"

"He means, when," Werner said.

"In any case, far enough in the past that we have neither radio navigation nor GPS," Christoph replied.

"Fly a curve. Let's see if we can see the wormhole!" Reuter said.

Christoph nodded and turned the heading knob on the autopilot until the aircraft started going down, making sure not to cross their previous course and accidentally fly into the wormhole. Although there was nothing he would have liked to do more than return to the present, he couldn't see the wormhole, and didn't want to risk flying only half of the plane through it.

With the help of the navigation display, which was now powered only by the inertial navigation system, Christoph steered the plane to within a mile of the wormhole, which was indicated by a big, red circle on the screen. "It should be just to our right."

Christoph followed Reuter's gaze out of the window. Even Werner leaned forward, gun in hand, to look outside.

"There's nothing there!" Christoph said in surprise. He had expected to see a circle of light, a blue vortex, or some other strange apparition hovering in the middle of the air, but outside was nothing but darkness.

"This is what we expected," Reuter said. "The optical distortion caused by the wormhole is too small. It's invisible to the naked eye. We would need the instruments to fly back through."

"Just as well we have the second capacitor. Stay on a southerly course until we reach Jade Bight, then we'll change to course one-five-seven."

"And what is our destination?" Christoph wanted to know.

Werner sat back down on the flight engineer's seat. "Munich," he answered sharply.

"Why Munich?" Reuter asked, barely able to suppress the anger in his voice.

"Because tomorrow evening, Adolf Hitler will be in the Bürgerbräukeller, delivering his annual speech commemorating the failed coup of 1923."

Christoph remembered. "The assassination attempt!" he blurted out.

Werner nodded. "Yes, the resistance fighter Georg Elser hid a bomb there to kill Hitler and all of the Nazi leadership. Unfortunately Hitler left early and the bomb exploded thirteen minutes too late.

"And you want to keep Hitler there until the bomb explodes?" Reuter asked in disbelief.

"No. Tonight, Georg Elser will go and check on the bomb that he planted there two days ago. We will intercept him in front of the Hofbräuhaus and make him set back the time fuse by half an hour."

Christoph shook his head. This was complete madness. It could never work. And yet ... if they really had traveled back to 1939? Yes, if ...

"How will we find out what the date is?" he asked.

"For flights further back in time we have a star sensor that can determine the exact date from the position of the stars," Reuter said. "But we don't have it on board today, since we only intended to travel twenty-four hours into the past." He looked sharply at Werner.

Werner smiled benignly. "Don't worry, we thought about that. Why do you think we have this good old-fashioned radio? After all, we have all the monitoring instruments on board that were supposed to be tested on the first mission. They include a run-of-the-mill radio.

Werner took a piece of paper from his breast pocket and placed it on the table in front of him. Then he pressed a button on his console and turned a knob next to it. A loud rustling noise could be heard from the loudspeaker. Werner turned down the volume slightly. "Let's see. Reichssender Hamburg. Medium wave nine hundred and four kilohertz." He turned another knob. "It should be here somewhere ..."

Suddenly classical music blared from the speaker. Werner turned down the volume. "There we are. The frequency is correct, at least. Now we just need to wait for the next news program."

"Even if we find out the correct time," Christoph began, "how do you want to find this Elster guy—"

"Elser," Werner corrected him. "Georg Elser. You should actually know his name. He's a hero. One of the few that existed in Germany at the time."

"Elser," Christoph repeated. "Whatever. We're sitting in an A380. We won't be able to land this plane at any airport. So what are you envisaging?"

"We won't land."

"We won't?"

"No. Max will jump out with a parachute."

"A parachute?" Christoph was bewildered.

"Yup. We're flying to Munich, where Max will jump out of the plane after pressure equalization. He'll take care of Elser and the bomb and we'll return to the present.

"Well, you seem to have thought of everything," Reuter said sarcastically.

"We have. We started planning months ago."

"We?"

"Max and I, and some other politically minded people."

"You're working for an organization?" Reuter asked.

"Not really. We're just a loose association of people who want to improve the world. I've known some of the members for years."

"That doesn't reflect well on the effectiveness of our security checks," Reuter remarked drily.

Christoph looked at the navigation display. "We're over Jade Bight now," he said, looking out of the cockpit window. From the left-hand side of the plane he could see the lights of Bremerhaven, and the illuminated area ahead of them must be Bremen.

"Then please change to course 157," Werner said in an exaggeratedly friendly tone.

Christoph hesitated a moment, sighed and turned the knob of the autopilot to the left. The aircraft reacted immediately.

The music coming from the loudspeaker stopped abruptly. A clear male voice was easy to hear above the rustling. "This is the Grossdeutsche Rundfunk. The High Command of the Armed Forces has announced that it has succeeded in securing and eliminating numerous resistance fighters in the south of Krakow."

Christoph could feel goose bumps on his skin. "The High Command of the Armed Forces ... my God! We really have traveled back to the Third Reich."

"Shhh!" Michael hissed.

"... yesterday a number of high-school teachers in

Krakow were arrested under suspicion of supporting the resistance. The traitors were sent to prison and are now awaiting trial. It is six o'clock. Berlin, November 7, 1939." The voice fell silent and music started playing again.

"My God, it worked!" murmured Werner hoarsely. "I almost didn't believe it would." He picked up the interphone and connected to the cabin. "Max! It worked. Get ready, in half an hour we'll be over Munich."

"My time machine," Reuter whispered. "It really worked."

"Werner seemed to know it would," Christoph said quietly. "What will happen if he carries out his plan and kills Hitler?"

Reuter shook his head. "I haven't a clue."

"Will there be a time paradox?"

"Possibly."

"And what happens then?"

"I don't know."

Christoph sighed again. He was convinced that Werner would trigger a catastrophe. "We have to stop him. We have to!"

"What are you talking about?" Werner asked and pointed his pistol at them.

"Werner!" said Christoph urgently. "We haven't the faintest idea what will happen if we change history."

"You're wrong. We can estimate fairly accurately what will happen."

"How can you say that?" Reuter asked. "It was the object of our research to find out the consequences of time paradoxes by changing very tiny things. What you're doing here is a massive interference with history."

"There are studies that deal with turning points in history," Werner said firmly. "A professor investigated this very case years ago: What would have happened if the assassination of Hitler had succeeded? The Second World War would never have taken place."

"As far as I remember, the Wehrmacht has already marched into Poland," Christoph said. "Several months ago! The war is well underway."

Werner shook his head. "The conflict is still confined. It will only really spread when Germany marches into Denmark and Norway next April, and then into the Benelux countries and France in May."

"And you think you can prevent all this with your crazy plan?"

"The studies suggest it would have been possible. When Hitler dies tomorrow in Munich with his inner circle, Germany will be left without a leader. A military government will take over command and as a result, both the spread of fighting and the mass extermination of the Jews—which was almost entirely Hitler's doing—won't happen. At the same time, Stalin's threat to the West will increase when he marches into Finland next year. This will force England to form an alliance with France, the USA, and then also Germany."

Reuter snorted. "We're already at war with England and France! Have you forgotten that?"

"There will be peace talks soon after Hitler and his henchmen are found dead. Germany will draw closer to the West again and fascism won't survive for long. The West will bypass the Second World War and move straight into the Cold War, which—like in our timeline—will come to an end at the end of the twentieth century. However without millions of dead on the battlefields or in concentration camps."

"That's pure speculation!" Christoph protested.

"It is a prognosis based on serious academic studies," retorted Werner.

"Insane! Absolutely insane!" Reuter shook his head.

"We'll see," Werner ended the discussion. "Where are we now?"

Christoph turned around to look at the navigation display. "We're already deep into Germany. Or I suppose I should say the German Reich! To our right is Würzburg. I can already see Nuremberg up ahead."

"Shouldn't they have us on their radars already?" Reuter asked. "I mean, the country is at war! Why aren't there any fighter planes on our tail?"

"Good question," Christoph answered. "I know that radar systems have been around since the start of the Second World War, but I can't say how good they are. If the radar system is already active, we would have been spotted over the North Sea as we approached the coast, but they're probably looking out less for individual planes than whole bomber squadrons." He looked out of the cockpit windows, nonetheless. "I think most aircraft at the start of the war would have had difficulty reaching our altitude and speed. The propeller aircraft of the time, like the Messerschmitt 109, probably couldn't fly much faster than three hundred miles an hour. Even if they have noticed us, they'll have trouble following us."

"I thought jet engines were used for the first time in World War II," Reuter said.

Christoph nodded. Like every other good pilot, he

had read up on aerial combat during the Second World War. "Yes, the Me 262, but they only came into service in 1944."

"We're not in any danger," explained Werner. "Nothing can stop our plan."

"Your plan is insane," Reuter spat at him.

Was it really? Christoph looked at Werner thoughtfully. What would happen if they really succeeded in killing Hitler? Was it possible that they could save millions of lives—here, today? Christoph shook his head. Messing around with history ... it couldn't be right. And what if they made things even worse? They had to stop Werner and his accomplices! Somehow.

"I need to go to the bathroom," Reuter said tonelessly.

Werner snorted. "Let's wait until we've flown over Munich."

"Are you telling me I can't go to the bathroom?"

Werner opened his mouth to make a retort, but then simply shrugged. "What the hell. I guess you can't do any harm in there. Go!"

Reuter supported himself on the back of his seat and clambered to the back. Werner stood up and stepped aside to let him pass. Reuter took a step toward the cockpit door. Then he spun round so fast, Christoph didn't have time to see what was happening, and threw himself on Werner.

Christoph jumped up. Jesus, he could have at least given him a sign! Reuter pushed the cursing Werner against the console. He hit his right arm. The hand holding the weapon crashed into a dashboard. A shot was fired, narrowly missing Christoph's ear. Werner took advantage of Reuter's state of shock to wriggle out of his grasp. He pushed Reuter off him and Reuter crashed into Christoph. Together they fell behind the pilot's seat. Christoph hit his head hard on something and cried out.

"Idiots!" Werner pointed his gun at them.

Christoph scrambled to his feet and searched for the spot where Werner's bullet had hit. He found it on the overhead instrument panel, just above the reset switches of the onboard electronics. If an important system had been damaged, or if the cabin pressure had dropped, there would have been a warning signal. It looked as if they'd been lucky, yet again.

Christoph was angry. It had been a rash thing to do, and could have cost all of them their lives. He sat back down on his seat just as Werner slapped Reuter in the face.

"Never try that again or I will shoot you. I swear it. Sit down!"

Christoph checked the instruments. Everything looked normal. Then his eyes fell on the navigation display. "Hey!" he exclaimed.

"What?" Werner asked quickly.

"The onboard electronics must have been affected. The inertial navigation isn't working." He could see the small aircraft symbol and their course was still being recorded, but the line ended several miles behind them. It didn't show any coordinates anymore, either. In other words: they didn't know exactly where they were.

"No big deal," Werner hissed. "We'll look for a fixed point over Munich and manually enter the coordinates." He gave a dismissive wave of the hand. "We'll think about it once we've dropped off Max."

He looked out of the window. "And that will be in just a few minutes. Look, Munich is ahead of us." He looked at Christoph sharply. "Set the altitude to six thousand feet. Then reduce speed with flaps fully up to just before the stalling point.

Christoph hesitated. Werner snorted, reached forward and turned the knob of the autopilot. "And now reduce speed!"

Feeling he had no choice, Christoph reduced the speed.

"Max, get ready. A few more minutes!" Werner shouted into the interphone. Then he turned back to Christoph. "Are you familiar with Munich?"

Christoph nodded.

"Good. Approach the Maximilianeum from the north. Max will jump out and land in the grounds to the south. From there it's only about a third of a mile to the Bürgerbräukeller. He'll have more than enough time to intercept Elser."

"And how the hell will you get him back on board?" Christoph asked, although he thought he knew the answer.

Werner confirmed his hunch. "He won't come back on board. He will stay in 1939. He is sacrificing himself for the good of the world."

"If the assassination succeeds, they will look for him and Elser. And you know what that will mean for him. Elser was caught back then, too."

"Not this time. Max is carrying forged papers for himself and for Elser. Both of them will make it safe and sound to Switzerland. From there, they'll travel to France, where they'll go into hiding until the time is right for them to be celebrated as heroes."

Christoph shook his head. It would never work in

a million years. Nevertheless, he followed Werner's orders and set the Airbus on a course that led straight to the Maximilianeum. The lights of the city were clearly visible, and he could make out the contours of the English Garden, which he used for orientation. It was hard for him to believe that the city he saw in front of him was Munich in 1939, and yet ... it was smaller than it was in the present day. Whole districts were missing. And the roads, which pulsated with traffic in the modern world, permanently congested snakes of light, were hardly visible from up here.

"Good! We're on course."

"Now flaps up and reduce the speed even more."

Christoph whistled through his teeth and carried out Werner's order. What else could he do? In the worst-case scenario, Werner would haul him out of his seat and fly the plane to its destination himself.

"Good," Werner said, satisfied. "Now equalize the pressure so we can open the door."

"Your guy will hit the front edge of the wing if he jumps out of the door," Reuter pointed out.

Werner laughed dismissively. "Not going this slow." He leaned forward again to look out of the window. "OK. Two more minutes. How's the pressure equalization?"

"Done," Christoph said.

"Max, you can open the door now. Two more minutes, I'll give the signal."

"OK, I'm ready," Max's voice came through the speaker.

Christoph switched to the lower fuselage camera. The night-vision imaging system gave him a good view of the buildings and streets of Munich. He found the coordinates of the Maximilianeum on the map and programmed them into the flight management system. After this improvised calibration, the inertial navigation would deliver at least halfway accurate values.

A warning signal blared through the cockpit. The front, lower exit door had been opened.

"That's the Maximilianeum!" Werner cried. "He grabbed the interphone. "Good luck, Max. You're already a hero! Jump in three, two, one. Go!"

On the screen, Christoph could see a human figure tumbling through the darkness until it was no more than a pinprick, which then disappeared.

This was insane!

"What happens now is no longer in our hands," Werner said calmly.

Christoph turned around.

His first officer handed him the pistol. "I apologize, and hand control of the aircraft back to you."

For a few seconds, Christoph could only stare in silence at this man whom he had so badly misjudged. He took the weapon from his hand, made sure it was secured, and stowed it under his seat. He picked up the interphone and switched it on to the cabin speakers. "Somebody please shut the door. And please could one of the cabin crew come to the cockpit to give us a status report."

Reuter tipped back his seat and pushed Werner aside, cursing. He leant forward over the console and studied the displays.

A few seconds later, the warning light for the exit door went out, and a buzzer sounded.

Christoph opened up, and Patrick, a young engineer, entered the cockpit.

"Everything OK back there?" Christoph asked.

"Sure, but that guy scared the hell out of us. Especially when he opened the door. I thought I wasn't seeing right. They must have manipulated the electronics in advance." Then he looked at Werner. "I didn't think you were such a complete asshole!"

"Did Max tell you what this is all about?" Christoph asked.

Patrick snorted. "Sure, he gave us a lecture on how he was going to save the world by killing Hitler. It'll never work!"

Christoph turned to Werner: "You haven't got any more surprises in store for us, have you?"

Werner shook his head and laughed. "No. My mission is complete. Now it's all up to Max."

"So you'll help me get this plane back home?"

"Sure."

Christoph indicated the seat next to him. "Then sit down and do your job."

"You don't actually trust him, do you?" Reuter was horrified.

"You heard him. He's achieved his goal. And I need a first officer."

Reuter snorted. He pointed a finger menacingly at Werner. "We'll talk later."

Werner didn't respond, and sat down in his original seat.

"Is the door at the back closed and secure?" Christoph asked Patrick.

"Yes."

Christoph turned to Werner. "We'll move up to flight level one fifty. Course three sixty."

Werner nodded. "OK."

Christoph checked to make sure Werner was

carrying out his orders correctly. A few seconds later the aircraft began to climb again.

"Now what?" Patrick asked.

"Now we'll return to the future using our time machine. Does it still have enough power left?"

Reuter studied the displays. "The second capacitor is fully charged."

"Then that's decided. We'll fly back to our test area over the North Sea."

Christoph checked the screens and saw to his satisfaction that they were heading north again. They had another hour's flight ahead of them to the test area. He was suddenly struck by a disturbing thought. "If we *were* spotted by the primitive radars of the German Reich, we can expect to have some fighter planes on our tail very soon." He turned to Reuter. "I would rather travel back to the future from somewhere else, in case we were spotted as we came in. Was the other exclusion zone over the Eifel in operation today?"

Reuter nodded. "Yes, for the whole test period. The NOTAMS have been active since last week. It's fine by me."

"Good, then let's try and get back to the future there. That will save us a few miles and at least half an hour."

Christoph calculated the route and set the autopilot to three hundred and six degrees. "We have another two hundred and fifty miles to our destination. About half an hour's flight time. Can you manage your calculations by then?"

Reuter nodded. "Yes. I'll program our time of departure in the past as our target time."

"Wait!" Christoph said. He didn't like the idea of

coming out in the dark over the Eifel, in case something went wrong again.

"What now?" Reuter asked.

"Can we change the target time so that we come out in daylight?"

His supervisor shook his head. "I could set the arrival time two hours before our departure, but then we would run the risk of creating a time paradox. We would land in Cologne before we started and meet ourselves."

"Interesting idea," said Patrick, who was still standing in the cockpit door. "We could prevent ourselves from taking off and foil Werner's and Max's plan."

Werner's eyes glinted in alarm. Maybe it hadn't been such a good idea to put him back in the first officer's seat. Christoph seriously wondered if Werner had it in him to crash the plane so that his plan wasn't jeopardized. He fumbled under the seat for the weapon.

But Reuter was shaking his head. "I wouldn't try it. To encounter yourself is the worst form of time paradox imaginable."

"Worse than what Werner and his accomplice have done?" Christoph asked. "It couldn't get much worse."

"We might really be able to prevent it in this way," said Patrick thoughtfully. "We could return a few hours earlier and land at the NATO base in Geilenkirchen. While we're still in the air we'll make contact with the airport and explain the situation. Werner and Max will be taken from the plane, and we will fly back to 1939 but without the plan of killing Hitler. We'll fly in a circle and like now, return over the Eifel. That way we would only exist in double for a short amount of time, and we could clear up this mess once and for all."

Reuter thought hard. "Might be worth a try. We'll prevent a big time paradox at the expense of a small one."

"I won't allow it!" Werner said calmly, his hands shooting forward in the direction of the sidestick. But Christoph had been expecting it and he hit him in the face with the butt of the pistol before he could do anything.

"Pull him out of the seat!" Christoph shouted.

Patrick and Reuter rushed forward and grabbed hold of the stunned Werner.

"Take him to the toilet and lock the door!"

Werner mumbled: "Don't do it! This is our chance to prevent the greatest crime in human history!"

Patrick dragged him out of the cockpit.

Christoph frowned. "Do you think he's right?"

"What do you mean?"

"Could we really prevent World War II if we let him carry out his plan?"

Reuter snorted. "Werner's an idiot! We have no idea of the consequences of a time paradox. That's why we started our series of experiments. If we find out that mistakes in history really can be avoided, then we'll do it.

Christoph thought for a moment and nodded. "OK. So shall we try the plan?"

"I'm in favor."

Christoph checked the navigation display. They had already covered most of the route and were just passing the Rhine north of Mannheim. When he looked out of the window, he could see the lights of

Frankfurt to the right. Again he was struck by how much darker the city was compared to the present day. Normally he would have been able to clearly see Frankfurt Airport from this distance, but there was nothing there. "Ten minutes until we reach the exclusion zone. Can you manage your calculations by then?"

"Yes," Reuter answered shortly and used his headset to make contact with his team in the cabin.

Christoph adjusted course again and programmed the onboard computer so that the plane would fly straight over the village of Adenau, which was in the middle of the airspace reserved for them. The aircraft changed course slightly to the left.

"Do we have enough fuel to keep circling?" Patrick asked, reappearing in the cockpit. "After all, we were only supposed to fly a loop over the North Sea."

Christoph waved his concern aside. "We had a full tank. We could stay in the air for hours if necessary. What's with Werner?"

Patrick grinned. "He's raging and banging against the toilet door. I locked it. He doesn't stand a chance."

"Done," Reuter said. "The time machine is programmed."

"Good," Christoph replied. "We're close to the target area. Three more minutes. Tell your team to fasten their seatbelts." He turned around. "The same goes for you, Patrick."

"Can I stay here? There's nothing for me to do back there."

"Sure, OK. Take Werner's seat. With those switches, you can push the seat back into a sitting position."

Patrick nodded and sat down.

"One more minute," Christoph said.

Reuter gave some final instructions to his team in the cabin, then got to work at his console. "Capacitor ready, injector and accelerator on. Oscillator ready. Green light from all stations."

Christoph checked all instruments one last time. "Altitude fifteen thousand feet. Speed in limits. Aircraft on course." He turned to look at the navigation display. "Another half a mile. Five seconds. Four, three ..."

Reuter and Patrick joined in the countdown. "Two, one ..."

20

Herbert stopped the jeep in the middle of a group of buildings. He pulled out the ignition key and got out of the car. His legs were weak and trembling. He hadn't eaten anything for over twenty-four hours. Slowly he approached the dilapidated office block. He had been here once before over ten years ago. With Gustav and Anne-Marie. They had found a storeroom of supplies in the cellar. Cans of food, biscuits, medication, even a few bottles of wine, and they'd stacked up as much as they could on the back of their vehicles. They'd planned to come back at some point to get the rest, but at the time the storeroom in the bunker was still well stocked, so they hadn't been in any hurry. Then some of his friends had died, and others had headed south. In the end, Herbert and his wife were the only ones left. They had forgotten about the supplies. But now he needed them.

The metal door with the broken glass pane in the middle was wide open and the frame had been bent. Herbert walked cautiously through the entrance hall. The ceiling had partially collapsed and pieces of plaster were strewn all over the floor. Pushed against the left wall, a green wooden table was quietly molding away. It smelled musty.

Herbert walked straight ahead to the stairs that led down to the cellar. They had already searched upstairs on their last visit. All they had found was office rooms with broken windows, anything useful had been rotted away over the years by humidity, wind, and weather.

It was dark in the cellar. Herbert pulled out his flashlight from his utility belt. There couldn't be much power left in the batteries, so he would have to hurry. He walked down the long corridor. The storeroom was at the far end, if he remembered correctly. Several doors, some of them open, led to the left, but he knew that he wouldn't find anything he could use there. Behind a closed door he heard the angry squeaking of rats—they had obviously been disturbed by his footsteps. Herbert hurried on, as fast as his hunger-ravaged body would allow.

When he finally reached the end of the corridor he pressed down the handle and pushed open the metal door with his foot. Carefully he entered the room and scanned it in the weak light of his flashlight. All hope drained from him.

At the back of the storeroom the ceiling and walls had collapsed. Earth and stones had fallen through the opening and now filled half the room. It was damp and cold. Scanning the room with his flashlight, he saw some rats lying dead between the remains of the torn boxes. He wouldn't find anything to eat here.

Slowly, Herbert turned around and staggered back along the corridor. It was over. He didn't stand a chance.

He climbed the stairs, crossed the entrance hall and stepped outside. Despite the sun and the mild temperature, he was shivering with cold, probably due to hunger. Eventually, he reached the jeep.

For a moment he looked at the other buildings of the deserted base and wondered whether he should search them, too. But he knew it was useless, they had made a thorough search all those years ago.

What could he do? He couldn't think of anywhere else nearby where it would be worth looking for food. The only chance of finding any intact buildings was to head further south, but by the time he had made his way through the devastated terrain, he would have starved to death. Perhaps the best thing would be to drive back to the bunker. Maybe he could summon up one last ounce of strength and dig another grave next to his wife's. Then he would lay himself inside it and wait for the end to come.

What was that? Herbert stopped in his tracks and listened. A thunderstorm? Unlikely at this time of day. And yet the sound reminded him of a storm. It quickly became louder and he suddenly knew what he was hearing.

And then he saw it. A plane! It was flying very low, straight toward him. A big jet, bigger than anything he had ever seen.

Herbert was rooted to the spot. Open-mouthed he stared at the gigantic aircraft. He wanted to wave, to cry for help, but he could only watch wordlessly as it flew over him and off into the distance.

Eventually he overcame his surprise. His mind was racing. So there were still humans somewhere! The plane was descending and flying directly toward the old airport. But surely that didn't exist anymore! And yet the aircraft was clearly coming in to land. The last thing Herbert saw before it disappeared from view was the wheels slowly emerging from the bottom of the plane. Then the noise of the engines subsided and came to a complete stop.

Herbert closed his eyes and shook his head in disbelief. Had he just imagined the last few minutes? Was acute hunger giving him hallucinations? No, he had seen the plane clearly.

If it had in fact landed, he should be able to reach it. It was his last chance of survival!

21

Suddenly it was broad daylight. At first, Christoph was so blinded by the light outside the cockpit windows, he had to close his eyes.

"Whoa ..." Patrick blinked.

Christoph lifted his hand to shield his eyes a little from the brightness. Luckily, his eyes quickly adapted to the new conditions. The first thing he looked at was the navigation display, on which he ought to be able to see the signatures of other aircraft outside the exclusion zone. But there was nothing.

"The radar must have been affected by the shot Werner fired. The GPS isn't working either," he said. He changed the frequency to the VOR of Cologne Airport, which was just fourty miles away. But he still didn't get a signal. "Strange," murmured Christoph. He turned on the radio and pressed the talk button on the microphone. "Langen Radar, XF39."

No answer.

"What is it?" Patrick asked.

Christoph leaned forward to look out of the window. About half a mile below them was a thin layer of cloud. Feeling uneasy now, he remembered that on the day of their departure there hadn't been a cloud in the sky. He turned around to Reuter. "Are you sure you've taken us back to the right time?"

He nodded. "Absolutely sure. Our trip back to 1939 confirmed that our calculations work. Why?"

"I don't have any other aircraft on my radar. I also can't make contact with Langen Radar, and Cologne isn't showing up on my screen, either. Plus we had better weather on the day of our departure." Christoph adjusted the frequency again. "I can't even hear the ATIS of Cologne Airport."

There was complete silence in the cockpit. There was no doubt: something had gone wrong. Christoph was sure they hadn't arrived in the present. At least not in the one they had left behind.

"There isn't a single fucking plane on the radar screen," he said, trying to suppress the panic rising up inside him. "And on every frequency I've tried there's absolute silence."

"If only we could see the ground," Patrick murmured.

"I'll go lower. Below the clouds. They can't be that thick," Christoph replied, setting the autopilot to six thousand feet. "And I'll change the course to sixty-five degrees. We're flying to Cologne."

"But we wanted to go to Geilenkirchen," Reuter said.

"I have no idea where or when we've come out," Christoph replied. "I'll fly to the nearest airport where we can land, and that's Cologne. Then we'll see."

"OK. Understood."

They flew into the layer of clouds, and were surrounded by gray. His heart pounding, Christoph adjusted the frequencies on the center instrument panel. "I've set the Cola VOR east of Cologne, which we're aiming for in our final approach."

"And?" Patrick asked.

"Dead," Christoph replied drily. Now they had emerged from the clouds and had a clear view of the ground.

"Yay!" Patrick cheered. "We're where we should be. There's the Rhine. It's all—" He fell silent.

Christoph raised his eyes and looked out of the window, too. Patrick was right. They were flying over the Ahr Hills and approaching the River Rhine, which wound its way like a shimmering snake into the distance. On the left, Rheinbach was clear to see. Christoph could make out the outer edges of the small town. But something about the picture was strange. The buildings lacked depth. The whole town was flat—as if somebody had neatly removed the houses and left only the foundations.

"It's in ruins!" Patrick whispered.

"What's the problem?" Reuter piped up. He unbuckled himself and leaned over Patrick. Then he turned pale.

"Oh my God! That's Bad Neuenahr-Ahrweiler! It's just a heap of stones!" he groaned.

Silently they stared out of the window as the plane reached its new altitude of six thousand feet. By now it ought to be possible to recognize individual houses, cars, and even people, but all Christoph could see was a dead, devastated world.

"Meckenheim ... Wachtberg!" Patrick had turned very pale. "My family is from this area. It's all been destroyed! There isn't a single house standing!"

"Over there is the Rhine. Oh my God, look at Königswinter!" Reuter said. His voice was trembling. "It's completely disappeared."

Christoph looked to the left. He could see Bad Godesberg and Bonn. But here, too, the same picture presented itself: either mountains of rubble or razed terrain. Now they were flying over the hills of the Siebengebirge.

"I'm making the final approach to Cologne Airport and veering left." Christoph was having trouble keeping the tremor out of his voice. He adjusted the autopilot and the plane went into a wide left curve.

"There! Uckerath, beyond it the Sieg valley and Eitorf. I went to the fair there last year with my girlfriend. Nothing but rubble." Patrick's voice was hardly more than a whisper.

The Airbus returned to a straight course. Visibility below the clouds was good.

"Hennef! Siegburg!" Patrick cried. "There isn't a single house left standing in any of the villages!"

"What happened?" Reuter groaned.

Cologne Airport came into view, including the runways. They were right on the extended centerline of runway 32R, although Christoph was struggling to spot the smaller 32L next to it. He couldn't see the crossing runway, either. Nor were there any approach lights. And the airport buildings were gone. Christoph stopped the descent at an altitude of three thousand feet. "I'll do a flyover first to check the condition of the runways."

"Damn it, what could have happened?" Reuter's face was pale.

"Werner and Max!" Christoph said. Anger was rising up inside him.

"What?" Patrick asked.

"Whatever Max did in 1939: this is the result. Germany is in ruins, and who knows how long it's been like this. It doesn't look as if there's anyone left alive."

"That can't be," Reuter whispered. He turned back to his console but struggled to focus on what he was doing. "I'll turn on the sensors. With the help of infrared, we should be able to see if there are any people down there."

They were getting closer and closer to the airport.

The asphalt on the runway was much darker than normal.

"The runway looks as if it's made of black glass," Patrick murmured. "Everything looks like after a war."

"War!" Christoph said. "Yes, like after a war. A nuclear war!"

Patrick stared at him open-mouthed. "Do you really think ...?"

Christoph nodded. "It looks like a hydrogen bomb exploded over the airport. The heat turned the asphalt into glass and the blast destroyed the buildings." He turned to Reuter. "Can you see anything on the infrared screen?"

"Nothing!" Reuter was on the verge of tears. "There's nobody still alive down there!"

"Get Werner from the toilet. I want him to see this."

Reuter nodded and left the cockpit.

They were flying over the airport now. Nothing looked familiar, Christoph realized. The 32R was considerably shorter than he knew it. Two miles long at most. The parallel runway didn't exist. Nor did the crossing runway. The foundations of the former buildings weren't where they ought to be. It looked as if the whole cargo area had never even existed— except for a pile of rubble at the western end of the runway.

"I have no idea if we can land here," he said to Patrick.

The engineer didn't reply. He was looking out of the window in a daze.

"Look out there," Reuter screamed, pushing Werner into the cockpit. "This is what you've done!"

The first officer leaned between Christoph and Patrick. Mouth agape and wide-eyed he looked out of the windows. "What is that?" he asked in a subdued voice. "Where are we? Is that ...?" He fell silent.

"Yes," Christoph answered. "That's Cologne. Or rather, what's remained of it."

"Will we be able to land here?" Reuter wanted to know.

Christoph had switched one of the screens to the lower fuselage camera and was examining the runway. "I'm worried we might skid on the slippery surface. I'm also not sure the runway is long enough. We've still got a lot of fuel in the tanks."

"Can't you dump some of it?" Patrick asked.

"I could, but I'd rather not. We might still need it."

"Could we fly somewhere else?" Reuter asked. "Maybe it's not this bad in other cities. We could try Frankfurt."

"I have my doubts," Christoph said. "I'm in favor of trying to land. We need to find out what happened. Then we can fly on."

"I agree—I think we should land," Patrick said.

"It isn't your decision to make!" Reuter snapped at the engineer. Then he took a deep breath. "But we don't have much choice. Alright, let's land," he continued in a calmer voice.

Christoph nodded. "I'll fly a big loop over Cologne and Bonn. Maybe we'll find an area that isn't as badly destroyed and can find out what happened here. Keep an eye on the images from the infrared camera. Surely there must be some people still alive."

The airport was behind them now, and they were heading toward the Rhine. Christoph changed the course to two hundred and ninety-two degrees, so that they would fly straight across the center of Cologne.

"That's where Vingst used to be, and Kalk over there," Patrick whispered. "All gone!" "As if the houses had disappeared into thin air."

"Too right," Christoph said grimly. "Several atomic bombs must have exploded over the city. The buildings were vaporized." He shook his head. Despite the shock, he was starting to think logically again. The city of Cologne had a population of one million people. If you counted the whole metropolitan area, considerably more. The nuclear explosion that had struck here must have killed all those people in a moment.

"Look! Down there!" Patrick screamed. "That's where the cathedral should be! It's completely disappeared!"

The engineer was right. The dark foundations of the cathedral were clearly visible next to the river Rhine. But not a single stone of the vast edifice was left standing. The whole city looked as if somebody had rubbed it out with a giant eraser. There was also no trace of the many bridges that had crossed the river.

"Anything on the infrared?" Christoph asked.

Reuter turned away from the window and returned to his console. "Nothing. There's nobody living here anymore."

Christoph steered the plane onto a south-easterly course, which took them past Bonn to the west. Then he would turn the plane around and go in to land. But did it make any sense to land, if there wasn't a building left standing anywhere in sight?

With the Rhine to their left, they left the

devastated city behind them and flew over the town of Wesseling. All that remained of the once flourishing refineries was a big, gray wasteland.

"What happened?" Werner asked, still starting out of the window with a blank expression on his face. "What the hell happened? Something must have gone very wrong!"

Patrick jerked his head around. "Something?" he screamed. "Look around, Werner! Everything has been destroyed! Cologne and Bonn have been wiped off the surface of the Earth. I'm guessing it looks like this all over Europe."

"If there was a nuclear war, then it must have been decades ago," Reuter said.

"What makes you say that?" Christoph wanted to know.

"We have radiation measuring instruments integrated into our sensors. I'm registering high gamma radiation. About one hundred millisieverts a day. But if a nuclear bomb had hit recently, the dosage would be much higher."

"One hundred millisieverts? Is that a lot?" Christoph was worried. "Is it safe for us to get out of the plane?"

Reuter shrugged. "For a day or two it's not too risky. If we had to stay longer, we would run the risk of getting cancer. Maybe even acute radiation syndrome."

"Any idea how long ago this atomic war was?"

Reuter shook his head. "I'm not a radiation physicist, so no, I don't know. Several years, decades maybe."

"But that can't be!" Werner whispered. "That simply can't be!" He grasped his face in his hands and tears rolled down his cheeks.

"Look, over there!" Patrick pointed out of the window at something on the left. "There's something still standing."

Christoph looked in the direction Patrick was pointing. He was right. Just to the east of Bonn, there was an area that hadn't been razed to the ground. Some buildings rose out of the rubble. They appeared to be badly damaged, but at least they were still standing. Christoph changed course to take them closer. "There doesn't seem to be anything left of Bonn, but it looks as if this suburb didn't take the brunt of the explosion."

"That's Hangelar," Patrick said. "You can see the airfield. To the south of it, some of the houses look as if they're halfway intact. I think that's the compound of the Federal Border Guard."

"What's your infrared screen showing?" Christoph asked.

"Hold on, I need to adjust the camera." Reuter tapped around on his console.

"Well?" Christoph urged. In a moment they would have flown past.

"Fuck. Nothing. All dead." Reuter sounded disappointed. Then he shouted. "Wait! There's something! There's a heat source between two buildings. I can see a vehicle. A jeep, I think. And the hood is warm. Hey ..." He rushed to the window. "I saw someone! Coming out of one of the houses, right next to the car."

Now Christoph saw it too. There was a jeep between two elongated buildings and next to it was a person. Christoph couldn't see the figure clearly, but it seemed to him as if he were looking up at them.

"So *somebody* is alive."

"Can we get his attention?"

Christoph shook his head. "We're not a fighter plane that can waggle its wings. But he must have seen us."

"We should land and search for him," Patrick said.

"Or her," Christoph added.

"Whatever. Hangelar isn't far from Cologne Airport. About six miles. We could be there in two hours on foot.

"Patrick's right," Reuter said. "Maybe we can find this person and get some answers."

Christoph nodded. "OK. We're nearly on the extended centerline of 32. Then I'll make our final approach." He glanced around and saw that Werner was huddled in a corner of the cockpit still crying. Christoph turned to Reuter. "Put him on the jump seat and strap him in. Then inform your people in the back. We'll be on the ground in ten minutes."

22

"It's pretty cold," Franka said, pulling up the zipper of her overalls.

"Forty-six degrees," Christoph said, and stretched out a hand to help her down the steep steps of the emergency stairs.

The landing had been surprisingly smooth. Luckily the glazed asphalt had given the tires enough grip, so that Christoph had been able to bring the plane to a smooth stop at the end of the runway. Then he'd shut off the engines and the APUs. It shouldn't be a problem to get the Airbus back up into the air. But where on earth would they fly to?

One after another, the crew disembarked the plane. Heated discussions broke out. Werner was standing a little to the side, a picture of misery. Christoph had only just been able to stop Dominik, the stocky mechanic, from beating Werner up.

He walked around the plane to inspect it, peered into the turbines, checked the wheels, brakes, and tail. Then he walked out in front of the aircraft and looked around. The runway was surrounded by shrubbery and wild grass. Beyond the boundaries of the airport, pine and oak trees towered into the sky. The nuclear war must have happened at least twenty years ago, if the trees in the Wahn Heath had already grown this big again. The Airbus looked completely out of place in this desolate, ghostly landscape.

Slowly, Christoph returned to the group. They had left several hours ago with ten people on board. After Max had jumped out of the plane over Munich, they were down to nine. Franka Weber, Dominik Bunde and the physicist Lars Riedel—who was responsible for the accelerator in the cabin—had joined Reuter, who was cursing loudly. Patrick Scheible, Horst Sendenhorst and Frederik Schröder were huddled together in another group, talking. Werner continued to stand to the side. Nobody wanted anything to do with him.

Christoph walked up to Reuter, who was still complaining about Werner and Max. He raised a hand and interrupted his superior. "That won't get us anywhere. What's happened has happened. The question is what we should do now. Whatever happens, we need to send a group to Hangelar to look for the person we saw from the air. And we shouldn't wait too long."

"Agreed," Reuter said, gradually calming down. "I'll go. Maybe with Patrick and Dominik?"

"I want to go too," Franka said decisively. "I want to know what happened."

"Alright," Christoph agreed. "I'll go, too. And we're going to take Werner. I don't want to leave him with the plane."

"Good. The rest of you can wait here."

"What if you don't make it back?" Horst asked anxiously. He was holding his clearly useless smartphone in his hand.

Christoph gave a wry laugh. "We'll be back. Who's going to stop us? There's nobody here anymore. We should be back in six hours, max, before it gets dark."

"What time is it, anyway?"

Christoph looked up. "The sun is in the southeast. I'm guessing it's about ten in the morning."

"Yes, that sounds about right," Reuter said. "I set the time machine for nine o'clock."

"So today really is today?" Franka asked hesitantly.

Reuter nodded and pursed his lips.

"This is no longer the world we left," Christoph said. "I didn't believe we could really create a time paradox. But unfortunately, Werner and Max have proven that it's possible."

"The question is," Franka interrupted, "what can we do to reverse it?"

"Nothing!" Reuter said flatly. "Even if we wanted to we couldn't. The capacitor banks are empty. We can't do any more time traveling."

"So we're really stranded in this changed present that we created?" Horst asked.

Reuter nodded without saying anything.

"My family! My parents! My sisters! They lived in Cologne." Horst looked at Reuter in horror. "And now they're dead? Just like that?"

Reuter looked down at the ground.

"We should have never built that infernal time machine," Franka murmured.

"If we hadn't done it, somebody else would have built one soon enough," Reuter retorted. But he didn't sound very convinced.

"It's too late for this discussion," Christoph said. "Let's go and find some answers." He turned to Reuter. "Do we have any equipment on board that it might be useful to take with us?"

Reuter shook his head. "Apart from the first-aid kit? No."

23

They left the aircraft and the rest of the team behind, and walked through the high, wild grass of Wahn Heath. After a few minutes they reached the forest surrounding the airport. Christoph noticed some hares, which bounded away at the sound of their approach. Evidently nature had recovered from the nuclear explosion. But humans and their world appeared to have been wiped out.

Christoph shook his head. In his own lifetime, the nuclear apocalypse had seemed immanent several times—the Cuban missile crisis in the early sixties being just one example. He tried to imagine how Hitler's death before the Second World War could have led to this result, but he didn't know enough about history to make more than a crude guess.

They trudged through the forest in silence. Christoph led the group with the compass built into his watch. He looked back and made sure Reuter, Patrick, Franka, and Dominik were following him. Werner trotted along, head hanging low, several feet behind them. After half an hour, they reached the edge of the forest. Beyond it were the remains of a village or suburb.

Christoph was horrified by what he saw. "Jesus! There's nothing left of the houses except the foundations." And even these had been turned into black glass.

"Where are we, anyway?" Dominik asked.

"I think this was once Troisdorf. The foundations are very big. Must have been an industrial site," Patrick answered. He looked around. "I thought there would be rubble lying around everywhere after a nuclear war, like you see in photos of the aftermath of the Second World War."

"No," Reuter said. "The shockwaves of an atomic explosion can produce an excess pressure of more than two hundred kilopascal. Everything is obliterated. The range of absolute destruction for a hydrogen bomb yielding twenty megatons is up to six miles. A single nuclear missile with several warheads would have been enough to flatten Cologne and Bonn and all the surrounding areas."

They made their way quickly through the industrial complex. As there was no rubble, they didn't have any obstacles to overcome. A few shrubs and young trees grew between the gaps in the exposed foundations.

Despite the cool wind, the sun gave off a pleasant warmth. From the surrounding trees came the sound of chirruping birds, which only emphasized the horror of the ghostly and devastated landscape—as if nature was making fun of the people who had erased themselves from the face of the earth.

A few minutes later they reached a wide road. The asphalt was still clearly visible, but like the runway it had turned into black glass. Beyond it they could see more foundations of buildings.

"I think this used to be Highway 8," Patrick said. "If we keep going south, we should reach the railway line soon."

The young engineer was right. A few minutes later they were standing in an area that must have once been a station. The bed of stones beneath the rails had fused together into a smooth surface. There was nothing left to see of the steel tracks themselves.

"The tracks were made of hardened steel!" Dominik exclaimed. "They can't have simply disappeared."

"Evaporated," Reuter said with a shrug.

"This is crazy!" Dominik cried. "I can't wrap my head around this. It's a fucking nightmare!" He dropped to his knees and started sobbing.

Christoph looked around. He couldn't see a single man-made edifice. The glazed track bed formed a straight line that disappeared somewhere on the horizon. He went up to Dominik and laid a hand gently on his shoulder. "Come on. We have to keep going." The mechanic blew his nose on the sleeve of his overalls and stood up slowly. His face was red and puffy.

Carefully they crossed the former tracks and passed through a residential area. It was harder to make headway here, as they had to be careful to avoid the holes of the former cellars of the terraced houses.

Patrick went up to one of the holes and peered down. His face turned pale. "Look at that!"

Christoph came up beside him. At first he didn't understand what Patrick was so upset about. The ceiling of the cellar must have vaporized, the ground had an eerie, black color. Only in one spot could the original concrete still be seen. Christoph gasped.

"My God!" he whispered. "It looks like the shadows of three people. Two big ones bending over a small one." He turned around to Reuter. "Do you think ...?" He trailed off as he saw tears welling up in Reuter's eyes.

"It must have been a family. Two adults and a little child," Reuter whispered. "They evaporated together with the ceiling of the cellar, but they shielded the floor from the radiation, which is why the concrete isn't glazed there."

Christoph turned around with a shudder. Was this all that remained of humanity? Shadows on the floors of ruined houses? Was this what it looked like all over Germany? What about the rest of the world? They had to find this person they had seen from the air!

A quarter of an hour later, they had left the residential area behind them. A little hill led down to the banks of a river. "Do we have to cross this?" Christoph asked.

"That's the Sieg River. I'm afraid so. Hangelar is on the other side," Patrick replied.

"I bet the water is freezing," Franka said.

"We have no choice," Christoph shrugged. "Look—over there it doesn't look that deep. Let's go."

He stepped up to the bank, took off his shoes and rolled up the legs of his pants as far as they would go. Franka was right. The water was freezing. But luckily, even when he reached the deepest part in the middle, it didn't go beyond his knees.

"So far, so lucky," Patrick remarked. "I used to go out on the Sieg in my canoe. Usually the water is much higher than this. It can't have rained much recently. The river often floods in the fall. Then we wouldn't have got across at all."

"Then we would have had to look for a bridge," Dominik said, wading out of the water on the other side.

"I doubt there's a bridge left standing anywhere around here," Reuter said.

Once they'd reached the other side, they put their shoes and socks back on, crossed a small meadow and climbed up a steep bank. From the top, they could see the foundations of another village or small town stretching miles into the distance.

"How far still?" Christoph asked.

Patrick looked around to get his bearings. "That's Menden; the Hangelar airstrip should be over there."

Christoph wanted to continue, but Patrick stopped dead in his tracks.

"What is it?"

"I don't get it," Patrick said.

"What don't you get?" Franka asked, coming up beside him.

"Where's the highway?"

"The highway?" Christoph asked.

"Yes. The A560 ran along this ridge. It led from the Sankt Augustin junction to Hennef. Right here." He dragged one of his shoes along the earth. "I mean, the nuclear explosion should have turned it into glass, like all the other roads, right?"

Christoph didn't have an answer. He didn't know the area around Cologne and Bonn that well.

"Maybe it was never built," Reuter said finally.

"Of course!" Franka said.

Reuter continued: "I'm sure a lot of things happened differently after Werner and Max's intervention in 1939. Maybe the highway was built somewhere else."

"I have another theory," Patrick said. "The A560 isn't that old. I think it was completed in the seventies or eighties. Maybe the nuclear strike took place before it could even be built."

"We'll only find out if we make it to Hangelar. Come on!" Christoph ended the discussion.

Gradually, their surroundings changed. They started to walk through an area in which some of the houses hadn't completely collapsed, although all that remained were empty shells. Stones, bricks and other debris littered the streets, which were blackened but not glazed. This made it harder to advance; several times they had to climb over piles of rubble.

"Strange—not everything was destroyed here, although it's right in the middle of an urban area," Christoph pondered. He almost fell headfirst down a heap of rubble and only managed to regain his balance just in time.

"Maybe a dud," Reuter said, sliding down behind him. "Or one of the MIRVs missed its target area."

"MIRV?" Christoph asked.

"One of the missile warheads."

"One of them? I thought every nuclear missile had just one warhead."

Reuter shook his head. "No, a MIRV ballistic missile can carry up to ten or more warheads which can be aimed independently at different targets."

"You seem to know a lot about nuclear missiles," Christoph said.

"A few years ago I was on a Ministry of Defense committee to discuss the possible nuclear armament of the Federal Armed Forces."

"Those things should have been banned after Hiroshima and Nagasaki," Christoph said. "I can't believe Germany was even thinking of deploying nuclear weapons."

Reuter shrugged. "The Allies had nuclear weapons stationed permanently in Germany. So it was nothing new. But when the USA became more isolationist and withdrew its warheads from Europe, the question naturally arose. They would have served purely as a deterrent."

Christoph laughed and drew his arm in a wide arc.

"As you can see, in this new present day, nuclear weapons weren't limited to being deterrents."

Reuter didn't reply.

They were making slower and slower progress. Suddenly the ground gave way under Dominik. Patrick quickly grabbed him by the collar and pulled him back. Thanks to his quick reaction, Dominik was saved from falling several feet down a manhole.

It had taken them half an hour to cover the last three hundred feet, but finally they reached a wide grassy area. This must be the airfield. The runway itself wasn't visible in the high grass. On the other side of the field they could see several hangars and buildings that didn't look too badly damaged.

"No sign of the person we saw from the air. God knows where he's gone," Reuter said.

"But let's keep going. Maybe we'll find out something inside one of those buildings," Christoph said.

They crossed the airfield and a few minutes later reached the runway.

"Looks in pretty good condition," Christoph commented.

"It's wider than I remember," Patrick added. "And longer, if I'm not mistaken."

"Maybe it had a different use than in our time."

"Look at that!" Patrick was pointing at something hidden in the tall grass.

Christoph stepped closer and saw the remains of a plane. "That's a tail. Not very big, it must have been a small plane. And look, there's also an engine."

"Maybe the plane was on the runway when the bomb exploded," Reuter said.

"Could be," Christoph replied.

"A business jet, maybe. They often took off from Hangelar."

"No." Christoph shook his head. "It was a military aircraft. That symbol is the aircraft cockade of the Luftwaffe." He studied the insignia more closely. "To be more precise, the Luftwaffe of the Wehrmacht."

"And there's a flag!" Patrick had walked round to the other side of the tail. "But what is it? It isn't the German flag."

Christoph joined Patrick. "Black, white, red. That's the flag of the German Reich."

"So National Socialism survived up until the nuclear war."

"Not necessarily," Reuter joined in. "The Nazis only used the old flag of the German Reich at the beginning; from the mid-1930s they used the swastika."

"And I know that in the Second World War they painted the swastika on all aircraft tails," Christoph added. "And there isn't one here."

"So I was right," Werner said. But there was no trace of triumph in his voice.

Christoph looked at him angrily. He could feel his hands balling into fists. "What did you say?"

"Hitler's henchman couldn't keep up his mission after the assassination."

Reuter ignored him. "After World War II we went back to the black-red-gold flag of the Weimar Republic. Maybe in the new course of time, they decided to restore the monarchy."

"Or there really was a new democracy and they just decided to keep the flag of the German Reich because it didn't have all the negative connotations that we associate with it now," Christoph said.

"Which means there wasn't a Second World War," Werner said.

"Take a look around," Reuter shouted him down. "What do you call this? There was a Second World War—with the impact of a Third World War!"

Werner pursed his lips and lowered his eyes.

"Let's take a look at the buildings. Maybe we'll find something," Christoph said.

The buildings were all built of brick. The roof of one of the hangars had collapsed, but the others had only suffered minor damage. Each of them was adorned with the symbol of the Luftwaffe, applied with white and black paint. All of the windows were broken.

"Looks like a military airport to me," Christoph said.

"Could be," Patrick agreed. "During the Second World War and beforehand, Hangelar was actually an air-force base. But after the war it was handed over to the Federal Border Guard."

Christoph walked over to a heavy steel door, which stood half open. He crossed over the threshold and into a hangar. Several fighter planes with jet engines were scattered around the hangar, tool trolleys at their sides. They must have been working on the aircraft when the apocalypse started. "Over there is an office. Let's take a look."

As they walked through the hangar, Christoph examined the planes more closely. They were fighter planes, without a doubt. But he had never seen ones like this. They resembled the American F-4 Phantom with their rectangular air intakes on the engines and the characteristic tails. The wreck they had seen outside had also been one of these. All of them were adorned with the cockade of the Reich Luftwaffe and the flag of the German Reich.

They approached another open door, on which "Management Office" was written in faded letters. Next to the door, a big window had been set into the wall. In front of it was a vending machine, which looked like it dated from the sixties. Patrick peered through the glass of the vending machine. "Afri-Cola and Reissdorf Kölsch. Looks like they didn't have a ban on alcohol during working hours." He reached his hand into a metal waste bin next to the vending machine and pulled out a bulbous beer bottle with a swing top, which must have contained at least a liter. It looked more like a wine bottle. "Bottled in 1968!" he said.

Christoph nodded. "Yes, somehow everything here is reminiscent of the 1960s. So the nuclear war was over forty years ago!" Carefully, he pushed open the door to the office. The shattered windows let in natural light. The room was about fifteen by fifteen feet and was filled with several desks. On one of them, Christoph spotted a black dial-up phone. Filing cabinets out of decaying plywood lined the walls. Christoph made his way slowly across the dusty room. Yellowed papers lay around on the desks.

Reuter and Franka followed him into the office. The young physicist opened one of the filing cabinets and pulled out a file. "These are maintenance manuals for engine parts," she said. "The pages are so moldy, it's almost impossible to make out the writing. And look, they fall apart as soon as you touch them."

Christoph stopped at one of the desks. He pulled at the handle of one of the drawers, but it came off in his hand. He dropped it and carefully tried the drawer underneath. It opened with difficulty. Inside were unopened cartons of cigarettes, a hip flask and some keys. And, still rolled together, a newspaper. "I've found something!" Christoph pulled the paper out of the draw and slowly unrolled it. The paper was also yellow, but it was dry and legible. He unfolded it and laid it front page up on the desk. The others hurried over and peered over his shoulder.

"WAR?" was the one-word headline covering half of the page.

"What kind of newspaper is this?" Franka asked. "Is it the *Blitz*?"

"No," Christoph said. "It's the *Cologne Express*."

"Read what it says" Reuter commanded.

"At least not it's not in a Gothic typeface," Christoph muttered, squinting at the small font under the headline. "As has long been feared, tensions between the Soviet Union and the United States have escalated into a nuclear exchange. After Soviet intercontinental missiles with nuclear weapons destroyed Honolulu, Anchorage, and bases on the Aleutian Islands, Washington was compelled to respond with a counterattack in which Vladivostok, Magadan, and military bases on the Kamchatka Peninsula were destroyed."

"America against the Soviet Union? That could have been part of our history," Franka said.

"Except that the Cuban missile crisis was about stationing Soviet missiles in the Gulf of Mexico. Here the conflict seems to have played out in the Pacific," Reuter said.

"The question is what Germany had to do with it," Patrick said.

"Read on!" Reuter urged.

"As Reich Chancellor Jochen Schuster announced, we stand firmly on the side of our American allies, and strongly condemn the escalation of the Japan conflict."

"Japan conflict? What's that about?" Patrick asked.

"No idea," Christoph retorted, without looking up from the page. "It's followed by lots of comments from German and European politician, but there's no further information on the background of the conflict."

"Reich Chancellor Jochen Schuster?" Franka mused.

"Never heard the name," said Reuter.

"From when is the paper?" Patrick asked.

Christoph looked for the date. It was right at the top of the page, next to the price. "Here. July 21, 1969."

"Somehow that date seems familiar," Dominik said from the doorway.

"I know why!" Reuter replied, turning pale again. "It's the day Neil Armstrong landed on the moon. A momentous day in the history of mankind."

Nobody spoke for a long time. Christoph stared down at the ground.

"And here it was the day humanity wiped itself out," Reuter broke the silence.

Christoph leafed through the thin pages and read the headlines. "It's all about the nuclear exchange between America and the Soviet Union, but without any details or background information. Here's a commentary warning of an imminent global nuclear war. At the end of the article, the writer recommends that readers keep their radios and TVs on at all times."

"We would need a history book to understand the events between 1939 and 1969," Franka said.

"I doubt we'll find anything like that here," Reuter responded.

"Still, we should search the other buildings," Christoph said.

They went outside. Christoph squinted in the bright sunlight. Then his heart skipped a beat. "Look!" he shouted. About sixty feet away from them was the jeep they had seen from the plane. A man was sitting in the driver's seat and watching them with the engine running, ready to make a swift escape.

"Wait! Don't drive away!" Christoph called out. He raised his hands to show that he was unarmed and slowly walked toward the man. "Stay where you are," he said to the others over his shoulder. "I don't want him to feel threatened."

He approached the jeep, but stopped about thirty feet in front of it. "My name is Christoph Wilder. We are unarmed. We would like to talk to you."

He couldn't see the face of the man in the car clearly, because the window was so dirty. Finally the man turned off the engine, got out of the car and cautiously approached Christoph. He looked around seventy and was very thin, emaciated in fact. His cheekbones stood out sharply under his pale skin. His gray hair reached to his shoulders. He was wearing beige cloth pants, which had a slight sheen, as if they were made of water-repellent material. A green, tattered parka reached almost to his knees.

"Are you from the plane that landed at Cologne Airport?"

Christoph nodded.

"Do you have anything to eat?" The man's voice

was trembling.

It dawned on Christoph that this man must be starving. He reached into his jacket pocket, took out a chocolate bar and handed it to the man. He stuffed the whole thing including the wrapper into his mouth and it was gone in a matter of seconds.

"Thank you!" he said and held out his hand to Christoph. "My name is Herbert Steinmann."

24

"Do you have any more to eat?"

Christoph turned around and gave the others a signal to come closer. "Has anyone got anything to eat with them?"

"I've got a sandwich from the galley in my backpack," Patrick said.

"Give it to him. His name is Herbert Steinmann."

Patrick rummaged through his backpack and fished out a sandwich wrapped in cling film. He unwrapped it and handed it to the old man, who took a big bite.

"I didn't think I would ever see another human being," Steinmann said at last, wiping some crumbs from his mouth with a trembling hand.

"Do you live here?" Christoph asked.

"Do you mean here on the base?" Steinmann sounded amused. "No. I come from a bunker complex nearby."

The man had an unusual intonation. The way he stressed his syllables was particularly odd. The German language had obviously developed differently in this other version of history—or perhaps simply hadn't changed at all since the middle of the last century.

"Are there other people living there?"

Steinmann shook his head. "No. I'm the last. All the others have disappeared or are dead. I was on my way to try my luck elsewhere."

Christoph swallowed. What kind of luck could you seek in this devastated world? "Radiation levels are still quite high."

"Yes. But what choice do I have when there's

nothing left to eat—at least not anything that isn't contaminated."

"How long have you been living in the bunker?" Franka asked.

"Since the war of course."

"Since 1969?"

"Precisely."

Franka looked at the old man with wide eyes. The others could also only look on silently as he stuffed the rest of the sandwich in his mouth. This man had been living for almost fifty years in a bunker? If Christoph had grown up in this world, he would have spent almost his entire life underground. He couldn't even begin to imagine what that must have been like.

"Are there no humans elsewhere?"

Steinmann laughed weakly. "Until today, I would have answered that question with 'No'. We were unable to make radio contact with other survivors for the last twenty years. But you are living proof that civilization still exists somewhere."

Christoph swallowed. Where should they tell this man they had come from? How could they tell him they were responsible for this apocalyptic world? When he looked at the stricken faces of his colleagues, he knew they felt the same way. It was probably best to tell him as little as possible. Steinmann probably wouldn't believe him anyway.

"What happened?" Dominik wanted to know.

"What do you mean? What do you think happened?" Steinmann asked, confused.

"He means," Reuter jumped in, "what do you think led to the nuclear war back then?"

Steinmann laughed. "You're asking *me*?"

Reuter nodded.

"Stupidity! Boundless stupidity."

"The Soviets?" Christoph asked, thinking of the newspaper headlines.

Steinmann shrugged. "I'm sure that's what some would say. But if you ask me, there are always at least two sides involved in every conflict. The USA and Europe also couldn't stop their saber-rattling. Instead of solving the Japanese question at the negotiating table, everyone just threatened each other. In the end, everyone's fingers were simply hovering too close to the red button."

That again. Christoph had no idea what he could be referring to. "The Japanese question?"

Steinmann eyed them suspiciously. "I'm not surprised that many things have been forgotten in this godforsaken world, but surely not what caused the final conflict that plunged the world into the abyss?"

Christoph didn't say anything.

"Now I have a question: Where do you come from?"

Christoph looked at Reuter. But he just shrugged.

Christoph turned back to Steinmann. "Let's just say we come from very far away."

Steinmann smiled weakly. "Judging by your futuristic-looking traveling companions and how well-fed you all seem to be, I can believe that. But in that case I wouldn't have expected you to speak such good German."

"Well, we are Germans, but from another country. We'd like to find out what happened to the people here," Christoph explained. He didn't quite succeed in keeping the uncertainty out of his voice.

"You founded an exiled government?" Steinmann asked.

"What do you mean?"

He nodded in the direction of Reuter. Only then did Christoph realize that the German flag was sewn onto their overalls. The upper arm was adorned with the black-red-gold stripes.

"The flag of the Weimar Republic," Steinmann pointed out. "I'm not as dumb as I may look. So, where have you made a new home for yourselves?"

"We can't say," Christoph was evasive.

"Why not?"

"For security reasons."

"Let me guess: the United States of America."

"And what makes you think that?"

"I can hear it in your accent."

Christoph was confused. Most people didn't notice his very slight accent. He had only spent a couple of years of his childhood in New York. But despite his age and the awful life he must have lived, this man was mentally on top form. "And if that were the case?"

"I would have assumed that the USA and the Soviet Union had borne the brunt of the devastation. I didn't think there would be any survivors there. At least not enough to build an aircraft like yours. What model is it? I've never seen one quite like it."

"We call it an Airbus A380," Patrick replied, unaware that Reuter was giving him an evil stare.

"Airbus?" Steinmann asked. "Never heard of it."

"It's a new company," Patrick said.

"Company?" Steinmann pursued. "So you still have a functioning economy?"

Christoph shrugged. They had to be careful not to contradict themselves in what they said. The old man would notice. He was already suspicious. "Listen. We came here to get information. We would really appreciate if you could answer our questions. Later we will tell you everything you need to know."

Now it was Steinmann's turn to shrug. He probably knew he had no choice if he didn't want to starve. "What do you want to know?"

"Everything!" Franka cried.

Steinmann gave her an irritated look.

"Above all, we want to know what happened in the world after 1939," Reuter said. Then he added: "From your point of view."

"Why 1939 specifically?" Steinmann asked.

"Because we only have incomplete records since that year," Franka stammered.

Steinmann scrutinized her. "You're welcome to accompany me to our bunker. We have a complete library on microfilm. And a lot of newspapers." He chuckled. "Only up to 1969, of course. Since then, we only have the logbook from our bunker, but I haven't kept that up for the last five years."

Christoph glanced over at Reuter. He nodded eagerly. "That sounds like a real treasure trove. We should get those records."

"And I would like to see the bunker," Christoph added. He still couldn't imagine how this man had lived underground for almost fifty years. "Where is it?"

"The bunker complex is in the hills of the Siebengebirge, under the Petersberg. About six miles from here. You're welcome to come with me in my jeep. We can be there in an hour."

"It's late already," Patrick pointed out.

Christoph looked toward the west. The sun was still above the horizon, but he was right: it would be dark in two hours.

"I suggest that Reuter and I accompany Mr. Steinmann to the bunker. We'll spend the night there and come to the airport after sunrise."

"And what do we do?" Franka asked.

"You go back to the plane and wait for us there. Or is it dangerous here at night?" he turned to Steinmann.

The old man shook his head. "In the seventies and eighties there were problems with plundering gangs from the Eifel region and Westerwald. To begin with, a lot of people survived down there in the valleys. But I imagine they're all dead by now. You should be safe on your plane. There's nobody living here anymore."

"Apart from you."

Steinmann laughed. "Only thanks to the bunker and all our supplies."

"Were there more bunkers?"

"Not many. There was one in the Eifel near Bad Neuenahr-Ahrweiler. We had radio contact in the early days. But it was looted years ago."

"Looted?" Reuter asked.

"Yes, one morning Hans—the radio operator—shouted for help. Gangs were invading the complex and had started to slaughter the survivors. A big group of us immediately made our way over to see what had happened. But all we found was dead bodies and plundered supply rooms."

"What a horrible world," Franka whispered.

"OK, well, we should get going, otherwise it will be too late," Reuter said. "Are you OK with the plan for the two of us to accompany you?"

Steinmann nodded. "Of course. If you want to know what happened in Germany, you'll find the answer in the bunker." He hesitated. "But I have one condition."

"What?" Reuter asked, but Christoph already knew the answer.

"If you fly away again, you have to take me with you!"

Fly away? Christoph thought. But where can we fly to in this devastated world?

25

"We're almost there," Steinmann said. He had skillfully maneuvered the jeep around all the obstacles in Hangelar until they reached the completely flattened area around Bonn. Slowly but steadily, they made their way across the black, glazed streets to the Rhine and turned off to the south. All of the villages to the south of Bonn, as far down as Königswinter, had been destroyed to their foundations.

Now Steinmann steered the vehicle to the left over the remnants of a smaller road into one of the valleys of the Siebengebirge hills.

"Didn't you say the bunker was under the Petersberg?" Reuter shouted from the back seat over the noise of the engine.

"Yes, that's right," Steinmann answered.

"But Petersberg is further to the south," Reuter shouted.

"You're right, the main access route was through Königswinter, but it caved in after the first nuclear strike. Since then we've used the secondary route through the Heisterbach Valley. We're almost there. To the left is the Dollendorfer Hardt. Petesberg itself is to our right."

Isn't that where the federal government used to have a guesthouse?" Christoph said without thinking. He bit his tongue.

"What federal government?" Steinmann asked blankly. "There used to be a spa hotel on the Petersberg. But of course that was also destroyed in 1969."

They continued on their way along a narrow road that ran between the mountains of the Siebengebirge.

It wasn't glazed but was crisscrossed with deep cracks and fissures. Occasionally they passed the remains of a houses. After a few minutes they reached a group of ruined buildings. Steinmann slowed down and turned off the road. To their left were the ruins of a big church.

"I know that ruin!" Reuter said. "That's the Heisterbach Monastery!"

"Yes, once upon a time," Steinmann confirmed and stopped the car. About three hundred feet further on, Christoph saw a tunnel entrance, which must be the entrance to the bunker.

"The old ruin on the left already looked like that before the war," Steinmann explained. "In the Middle Ages it was one of the most important churches in the country and belonged to the Order of the Cistercians. But the abbey was secularized in the early nineteenth century and the church was used as a quarry—to build Ehrenbreitstein Fortress near Koblenz, for example. By the time a religious order reclaimed it after many years, the church had fallen into ruin. The other buildings were destroyed in the war. We—the inhabitants of the bunker, that is—created a cemetery there. Two days ago I buried my wife there."

Christoph swallowed hard. "You lost your wife two days ago?"

"No," Steinmann said in a sad voice. "She died ten days ago. But it took me a long time to dig the grave, since I was all alone."

"What did she die of?" Reuter asked.

"Cancer, I suspect," Steinmann said flatly.

"You suspect?"

"I'm not a doctor, and nor was my wife. Since

many people in our community died of cancer, I'm guessing that it was also the cause of my wife's death."

Steinmann put the car back in gear and drove to the entrance of the tunnel, finally coming to a halt in front of a set of heavy steel gates. Next to it was a rusted sign on which the writing was no longer legible.

"What was this bunker used for in the past? I mean, who operated it?" Christoph asked.

"In the early sixties, Bonn built an emergency bunker for the Gauleitung."

"And you belonged to this ... Gauleitung? Like a regional government?"

"Correct. I worked as Secretary to the Gauleiter of Cologne-Aachen, which is why my wife and I were in the bunker when the war started. I can still clearly remember how, a day before, the USA and the Soviet Union exchanged their first blows in the Pacific. We made our way straight here from Cologne. As soon as we'd closed the doors behind us, the earth shook. The bunker entrance in Königswinter collapsed, and the radioactivity in the Heisterbach Valley was so high, it was ten years before we dared to leave the bunker and saw daylight again."

The entrance to the bunker looked like any tunnel entrance, but it had been secured with a gate. There was also a smaller door integrated into the gate, so people could get in and out more easily.

"Could one of you please open the gate?" Steinmann asked. "You're younger and stronger."

"Of course," Christoph said and jumped out of the jeep. "How do I get it open?"

"There's a metal flap in the concrete wall next to

the gate. Open it."

Christoph found the flap immediately and pulled it up with a lever. Behind it was a steel wheel with a lever on it.

"Turn the wheel counter-clockwise."

The wheel was surprisingly easy to move. Slowly and without creaking, the gate rose up.

"That's enough. You can get back in."

Christoph climbed back into the jeep. Steinmann put the car into gear with a crunching noise. The jeep jerked into motion. The old man switched on the headlamps as they entered the darkness. The lights illuminated the ground and walls of the tunnel directly in front of them, but the end of the tunnel was nowhere in sight.

"How long is this tunnel?" Reuter asked.

"About half a mile. Then we get to the garage with the airlock."

"And you just leave the gate open?"

"There's nobody left to attack us," Steinmann said. "That wasn't the case in the old days."

"Was it bad?"

"During the early years we were constantly under siege. First it was survivors from down in the valley, whose homes had been destroyed."

"What did you do?"

"We let some of them in, until our air-filter capacities were exhausted. We decontaminated the newcomers, but without exception, all of them died of radiation poisoning within a few days or weeks."

"But you said you were under siege for years?" Reuter persisted.

Steinmann nodded. "After the first wave, there was nothing for several months. Then suddenly people started turning up again. They had survived deep in the Westerwald region, which hadn't been hit directly, and they weren't as badly radiated as the first wave of people. But civilization as we knew it had fallen apart, it was a lawless free-for-all. Survivors banded together into gangs and pillaged what remained of the cities. Those who tried to resist the gangs were massacred, or worse."

"Worse?" Christoph asked. He wasn't sure if he wanted to hear the rest.

"We watched it on the screens in our control room," Steinmann said in a trembling voice. "They camped outside the entrance to our bunker but couldn't open it. They killed each other and ..."

His voice cracked.

"I mean, they turned into cannibals. Hunger must have driven them insane."

Christoph didn't say anything. Could this really be true? Was civilized society just an atomic bomb away from the abyss?

"Finally, the gangs disappeared too. They died of the aftereffects of radiation or simply starved to death."

They had reached the end of the tunnel—a ten-foot-high wall out of concrete. On the right was a big rolling gate, which was open, and to the left of it a steel door. Slowly Steinmann drove through the gate into a garage, where there were two more vehicles and several high shelves filled with tools, engine parts and metal canisters.

"We're here," Steinmann said and turned off the engine. "Normally we'd have to decontaminate the jeep now, but since we're leaving tomorrow morning, it's hardly worth it. Come with me, I'll give you a tour of the complex." With difficulty, he climbed out of the driver's seat and walked slowly to the back of the room. Christoph and Reuter followed him.

"It's straight ahead to the storeroom. There isn't much left there, unfortunately. No more food. Until we get back to the plane we'll have to fast."

We'll survive, Christoph thought. In any case, he'd lost his appetite since arriving in this new present.

Steinmann opened a door. Christoph followed him into a long corridor, which was dimly lit by ceiling lamps. The walls were a greenish-gray color, which gave the place a depressing atmosphere. It was cold and musty. The humidity in here must be very high. Had Steinmann really spent almost his whole life in this dungeon?

"How do you get electricity?" Reuter asked.

"We have several generators in the supply room. And we had more than enough diesel to keep them running—we were able to help ourselves from surviving gas stations in the area. Air and water are cleaned and treated using simple filter systems. Wastewater is channeled outside via a sewage system."

They followed Steinmann through the corridor, past several solid steel doors. "On the left are the offices of the Gauleitung staff. And on the right are more storerooms. Here, on your left, is our small infirmary, which even has an operating table and operating instruments."

"You had a doctor in your group?" Reuter asked.

Steinmann nodded. "Dr. Fischer, yes. He was the first one to die."

"How?"

"He was stabbed by a survivor from outside whom

he'd wanted to help. He bled to death in front of our eyes."

Had there been anything but horror and misery in this world?

"How many people lived here?" Reuter asked.

"To begin with there were fifty-six of us. Fewer and fewer over the years. After ten years, we were down to forty-five, after twenty years there were just thirty of us left. Then a group of twelve people set off for the south, and the rest either died or disappeared."

"What were the people who left hoping to find in the south?"

"We presumed there had been less strikes in southern Europe. At least that's what we could gather from radio contact in the early days. But personally, I think the nuclear radiation spread across the whole planet. Maybe the southern hemisphere got off more lightly, partly because there weren't as many targets, and partly because the Innertropical Convergence Zone forms a natural barrier to the spread of radiation. But since we were never able to make contact, we can't know for sure.

"And you haven't had contact with anybody else— besides the people in that bunker in the Eifel?"

"Some at the beginning. But only locally. The radiation in the atmosphere blocked long-wave radio signals. But our radio hasn't worked for twenty years now.

They had reached a fork in the corridor.

"To the left are the engine rooms with the filters and generators. Through this door is our dining area and adjoining kitchen. We used to have an emergency exit in there—some steps led up into the cellar of the hotel on the top of the Petersberg, but it caved in following the nuclear strike." Steinmann continued walking along the right-hand passage. "Here on the left are the living quarters. If you carry on along the passage you get to an airlock, which used to lead to the tunnel exit in Königswinter, but as I said, that was destroyed."

He stopped in front of another steel door that was slightly ajar. Light fell through the narrow crack. "Here you will find your answers. This is the central office with the archives."

Steinmann opened the door and stepped inside. Christoph and Reuter followed him. The walls were lined with old-fashioned consoles that looked like relics from the Cold War. They reminded Christoph of photos he had seen of abandoned nuclear missile bases. In front of the consoles, scruffy leather chairs were attached to the ground. "This was the control room. We could monitor the bunker itself and the area outside the gates on the screens."

At the back of the room were cupboards and a wide table with a contraption that looked like a huge, early computer. "There in the cupboard are the archives. You'll find everything you need on microfilm."

"Did you also archive daily papers?" Reuter asked.

"Only the Year-in-Review editions." Steinmann opened a drawer and took out several microfilm cards. He looked at the label and nodded. "1939. That's what you were looking for, wasn't it?"

"Yes, perfect," Reuter said. "Can you explain how the reading device works?"

"Of course." Steinmann slipped the microfilm card into a slot on a machine on a table, and tightened a screw. Then he flipped the switch. "Oh!" he said.

"What's the matter?" Christoph asked.

Steinmann stood up. "I'm sorry. The bulb must have given up the ghost."

Reuter groaned. "Don't you have any spare bulbs?"

Steinmann shook his head. "No, that was the last one. Although we haven't used this machine for at least twenty years."

"Shit," Reuter said.

Steinmann didn't seem too concerned. "You can take the films with you and analyze them at home in the USA."

Christoph exchanged a glance with Reuter. Would Steinmann be able to accept the truth? That they were time travelers who had changed the course of history in 1939 and were responsible for this nightmarish present? He didn't think so. A feeling of desperation welled up in Christoph. "What are we going to do now?"

"Go back to the plane," Reuter answered.

Steinmann shook his head. "Not today. It'll be getting dark outside. Driving at night is too dangerous."

"Didn't you say there were no other people alive?" Reuter sounded worried.

"Yes, but it's too dark. And we would have to cross the Sieg at a ford. I can only do that in daylight. We'll spend the night here and leave at dawn." He turned around. "Follow me, we'll go to the dining room. I'll get you blankets from the storeroom. And somewhere there ought to be a bottle of schnapps—that should warm you up a bit."

"God, in this depressing place, I can't believe he

didn't finish it all off years ago," Reuter mumbled.

Steinmann must have heard the cynical comment, but he didn't respond. "Since you are so curious, I would be happy to tell you what happened here. My wife and I have always believed in the importance of education, so I ought to be able to answer at least some of your questions, if you think that might help?"

26

"Adolf Hitler," Reuter said.

Steinmann stared at him for moment, then nodded. "What do you want to know about him?"

They had arrived in the dining room, which resembled a canteen, with two long tables and a hatch for serving food. The chairs were uncomfortable and the room was cold. Christoph decided to have a little of the cognac. It scratched his throat when he swallowed, and the warmth in his stomach quickly died away. All that remained was a faint feeling of nausea, but at least it gave him a little distance from the hardly bearable events and discoveries of the day.

"Can you tell us about his death?" Christoph asked.

Steinmann leaned back in his chair slowly. Christoph had the sudden feeling—not for the first time—that he had met the man before, but of course that was impossible.

The old man took a sip from his glass and put it back on the table. "November 8, 1939. A day no German will ever forget. He was giving his annual speech commemorating the failed coup when he was assassinated—blown up by a bomb that exploded right behind his back." He frowned. "Don't tell me you didn't know about that?"

"Of course we know," Christoph replied. "We're simply interested in hearing your interpretation of events."

"Is this some kind of test?" Steinmann asked skeptically.

"Trust me," Christoph explained. "It isn't a test. We just want to hear your perspective. If you knew our story you'd understand."

"Then tell me your story!"

Christoph didn't say anything. Reuter also didn't say a word.

Steinmann sighed. "What the hell. It's general knowledge, anyway." He reached for his glass. "So, Hitler was dead. Along with five hundred other people who were trampled to death trying to escape the Bürgerbräukeller as it collapsed. Including almost all the head honchos of his government: Himmler, Goebbels, Bormann, Hess, Ribbentrop, and many more.

"What happened then?" Christoph asked.

"The whole country was in a state of shock. Nobody knew what would happen next. Reich Minister Göring took over the leadership and ordered a retaliatory strike the following day—sent a squadron of bombers to London."

"Why London?" Christoph asked.

"Because everyone assumed the assassin was a British agent."

"So the assassin wasn't caught?"

"The name of the bomb-maker—Georg Elser, as I'm sure you know—was made public that night. The whole of Germany was up in arms and a massive manhunt began. The next day it was announced that he had probably escaped to Switzerland via Constance under a false name and with an accomplice. The two of them were never found."

"With an accomplice ..." Reuter muttered.

"What happened then?" Christoph asked.

Steinmann shrugged. "Göring tried to take over as leader but he didn't have Hitler's charisma or strategic and political capabilities. Above all, he was accused of being indecisive. To counter that, he made a half-hearted and ultimately pointless attack on French positions in Alsace, which claimed the lives of tens of thousands of German soldiers, since his beloved Luftwaffe had been unable to take out the enemy. That led to a coup in summer 1941 by senior military officials, including Rommel and von Witzleben, who removed Göring from the Chancellery. Just a few days later, the Soviet Union under Stalin invaded western Poland and eastern Prussia. The advance of their troops could only be stopped at the Oder River. Von Witzleben, who had provisionally taken over the affairs of state, was forced to negotiate a truce with the France and England, to prevent a war on two fronts. Several forays were made by German as well as by Soviet forces, but none of them led to a decisive outcome despite heavy losses on both sides. It was reminiscent of the dreadful trench warfare during the Great War."

Christoph listened open-mouthed. It was fascinating and terrifying at the same time, to hear how history had taken a different course.

"Meanwhile, in Asia, Japanese forces, which had previously occupied Manchuria, invaded the Soviet Union and captured Vladivostok," Steinmann continued. "Stalin decided not to advance any further on Germany but to transfer his troops to East Asia. That war ended in 1945 with the capture of Hokkaido by Soviet forces. The Japanese put up a strong resistance, but the Soviets massacred the population on a massive scale. Finally, the Japanese were forced into entering an alliance with the USA, who saw their supremacy in the Pacific threatened by the Soviet Union."

"Wait," Christoph said. "The US wasn't involved in military action at the time?"

"No, some had wanted to intervene in Europe on the side of France and England, but following the ceasefire, there was no longer any need."

"And what happened in the Pacific? I mean Pearl Harbor?"

"Pearl Harbor? What's that?" Steinmann asked in confusion.

"Didn't the Japanese attack America on Hawaii?" Reuter asked.

Steinmann shook his head. "No, the Japanese focused their imperialist policies on the Asian continent."

Christoph and Reuter exchanged glances.

"It's like you really have come from another planet!" Steinmann said. "You don't seem to know much about history."

Reuter ignored his comment and asked: "What happened next?"

"There were ceasefire agreements, but nobody trusted the peace. The conflicts hadn't really been resolved, and everyone was afraid that a major war hadn't been averted, but simply postponed. And the major powers prepared themselves for this coming war."

"They developed nuclear weapons," Christoph stated.

"Yes, after it became known that the USA, thanks to Dr. Teller, was going to great lengths to develop and construct nuclear weapons, comparable programs were started in Germany under Heisenberg and in the Soviet Union under Kurchatov. In the autumn of 1950, all three countries carried out successful tests, which started the arms race."

"What was going on in Germany at the time?"

"When it seemed like the fragile peace of the mid-forties was holding, the military government under Witzleben finally approved free democratic elections. That at least led to a peace treaty with France, England, and the United States. But the DNSP—the German National Socialist Party—won the election by a landslide and installed Hans Frank as leader. And he wanted to return to the Führer principle as soon as possible. The fifties were a difficult decade, with a series of autocratic governments which were successively removed by military coups. Finally, the Wehrmacht made another attempt to establish a democratic constitution, and parties that opposed it weren't allowed to stand for election at all. It was only in the sixties that a bit of prosperity returned to the country. However, the threat of global war arose again—the USA and the Soviet Union were carrying out several proxy wars all over the world. The USSR, in particular, ruthlessly pursued its interests after Stalin's death."

"After Stalin's death? You mean under Khrushchev?"

Steinmann laughed. "Khrushchev? Are you joking? He only survived Stalin by two days."

"But who—?"

"Beria!" Steinmann answered.

"Lavrentiy Beria? The mass murderer?" Reuter whispered.

"The very one. The former head of the Secret Services. It was said that he poisoned Stalin and Khrushchev with his own hands in order to finally come to power. Many people said he'd gone mad, and when you consider how many times he threatened the USA and the German Reich with nuclear strikes, there might be some truth to those claims. I'm still convinced that he was the one who fired the first nuclear missiles at the US in the fight for Japan. Since the German Reich had entered into an alliance with the United States a few months earlier, Chancellor Schuster had to start deploying nuclear weapons, too. But by then, Soviet medium-range weapons were already on their way to us."

27

"Crazy ... The story he's telling us bears hardly any relation to the world we grew up in," Christoph had lowered his voice. Steinmann had gone out to prepare some beds for his guests.

"That's not quite true," Reuter said thoughtfully. "If you take a step back, you'll find parallels. There was armed conflict in the 1940s here too, but it didn't develop into a global war. As far as that goes, Werner and Max really did succeed. By eliminating Hitler, they saved humanity from the Second World War. But they—and whoever else was behind the plan—didn't consider one thing."

"What's that?" Christoph asked.

"The atomic bomb," said Reuter. "Either Werner didn't think about this ultimate weapon of destruction or he assumed it would never be built without the Nazi threat. But he was wrong. It just happened a few years later. Developed by the USA, USSR, and German Reich simultaneously. With fatal consequences."

"I don't understand," Christoph said. "In our history, too, giant nuclear arsenals have been built as deterrents—but never used. Why's that different here?"

"Hiroshima and Nagasaki," Reuter said.

"What do you mean?"

"In our history, the atomic bomb was developed in the Manhattan Project in the late stages of the Second World War. Apart from the test bomb that was detonated over New Mexico, there were only two that could be used against the enemy before the war ended. The whole world saw what happened to those cities: it was horrific, and it served as a deterrent to using them again later. And Europe lying in ruins was a clear warning of what awaited humanity if another global conflict broke out. The change to the course of history meant there was no warning sign, and fingers were more prepared to press that red button." He shook his head. "Werner saved millions of lives with what he did. But as a result he wiped out all of humanity."

"What can we do?" Christoph asked.

Reuter groaned. "I don't know."

"We have to go back to 1939!"

"The capacitor is out of power, remember? We can't go back in time again."

"Then we'll have to fly through the wormhole. It must be visible above the Eifel."

"Yes, for about another thirty-six hours. But what do we do then?"

"We stop Max making contact with Elser."

"It's too late for that. If we fly through the wormhole tomorrow, it'll be a day later in 1939, too. The wormhole mouths move in parallel with our time. Elser will have already charged the fuse on his bomb."

"We could send a radio message and warn them of the impending attack. That way we would save Hitler's life."

Reuter frowned at him. Christoph also couldn't believe what he was saying. Of course they might restore the old course of history, but did he really want to save Hitler's life? The idea was absurd. Almost any other human being, for sure—but one of the greatest criminals in human history? And then live with the knowledge that this dictator would lead the world into war? Wouldn't that make Christoph partly responsible for millions of victims? Was that the price they had to pay to have a chance at a future? He stared at the ground in silence, lost in thought. A few minutes later, Steinmann entered the room again.

"Your rooms are ready. It's getting late. I suggest we get some sleep, so that we can get to the plane early tomorrow."

"Wait," Christoph said. "I still have a couple of questions."

Steinmann sighed, returned slowly to his chair and sat down opposite Christoph. "Alright. What do you want to know?"

"What about you?" Christoph asked. "What's your story?"

"My story?" Steinmann repeated. "I already told you how I ended up in the bunker and what life was like here."

"When were you born?" Reuter asked.

"September 20, 1939. Not far from here. I studied law in Cologne and married young. We lived in Cologne, where I worked in the Gauleitung."

"A Gau was a Nazi party administrative district, right? And its leaders were members of the SA or SS, if I remember rightly. So—"

Steinmann interrupted him. "The SA and SS were both banned in the forties after one of the putsches. The Gaus were turned into civil administration units of the German Reich. The Gauleiter were elected by the people and most of the staff was made up of party-independent officials like myself."

"Why was the name 'German Reich' never changed?" Christoph asked.

Steinmann looked at him blankly. "Why would we

have done that?"

"Never mind."

"What do you think would have happened if Hitler hadn't been killed?" Reuter asked.

Steinmann laughed weakly. "We often asked ourselves that over the years. Many people thought the German Reich would have fared better and that Hitler would have been able to keep Stalin in check. I'm sure the political turmoil in Germany in the forties would have been avoided. Many people also thought the German Reich under Hitler might have gained supremacy in Europe if the plan to conquer France via the Benelux countries had been carried out. But those are just idle speculations, because nobody can know."

"What do *you* think?" Christoph asked.

"What I think?" Steinmann picked up his glass. "I think that Hitler was a megalomaniac and so was his whole administration. He wouldn't have hesitated in leading Europe into a war of annihilation in order to fulfill his ambitions. America would have been forced to enter the war, would have developed an atomic bomb on a fast-track program, and would have bombed Germany. In the end, we would have ended up where we are today, just faster. I don't think humans can hold such power in their hands without destroying themselves." He looked at Reuter and Christoph in turn. "I'm tired. Do you mind if I go to bed now?"

"One more question," Reuter said.

Steinmann nodded.

"What happened to the Jews?"

Steinmann looked at him in confusion but finally nodded. "Yes, I see what you're getting at, since you keep talking about Hitler. In the thirties, anti-Jewish sentiments were strong and there were some attacks. Some Jews were even taken to concentration camps. But after the Wehrmacht overthrew Göring, those repressive measures were fortunately lifted. Later, it was found out that Hitler had secret plans to move all Jews onto a kind of reservation. Others believe it might have been far worse, but who knows."

Christoph exchanged a glance with Reuter. It was an absurd situation. Maybe they really could fly back to 1939 through the wormhole, prevent the assassination of Hitler and restore the old course of history. But it would be at the expense of millions of lives—people who, in this world, at least, had continued to live until 1969. Did they have the right to decide their fates? Could the victims of Hitler's vile policies be offset against the billions of people who would otherwise die in a nuclear war? It was crazy to think they were even in a position to make this decision. The damn time machine! If only Reuter had never built it!

28

"My darling," Steinmann said quietly, gently stroking the wooden cross. "This is the last time I'll be able to visit you. I've found a group of people I can join, and I hope to get to a better place with them. I thought I would remain here in this peaceful spot beside you for eternity, but I have to seize this opportunity—I hope you understand."

Christoph and Reuter were standing a few feet behind Steinmann looking at the row of wooden crosses. To their right was the former monastery, now a moss-covered ruin.

Christoph had hardly slept a wink. It had been cold and damp and he had shivered all night, despite the blanket Steinmann had given him. His also hadn't been able to stop thinking about everything they had spoken of the night before. He wanted to talk it over with Reuter, but so far this morning there hadn't been an opportunity to speak alone. Maybe now was a good moment? He turned around and pulled Reuter with him toward the ruined monastery.

"The way I see it, we have two options," he began. "The plane has enough fuel to fly another four hours. We could fly back through the wormhole to 1939 and try to save Hitler, awful as that sounds. The other option would be to stay here and try and use the remaining fuel to get somewhere where there are still people alive."

"You heard what Steinmann said," Reuter hissed. "The whole world has probably been destroyed. I'm not staying here!"

"So we save Hitler, accept all the deaths of the Second World War, and try and get home," Christoph concluded. He thought of his family. His son. His grandson. He couldn't bear to imagine how they would have fared in this apocalyptic world. That is, if they had been born at all. His own parents had only met because his father had been stationed in Germany as an American soldier. Probably he, Christoph, would never have existed in this godforsaken world. But wasn't that also a kind of time paradox? If he had never existed, how could he have flown back in time and involuntarily supported the assassination of Hitler? His head started spinning when he thought about it. "If we do it, how should we go about it?"

"We'll fly back through the wormhole and warn the Nazis via radio about the bomb in the Bürgerbräukeller," Reuter replied.

"And then?" 1939 will be our final destination. So what do we do? End up in Nazi Germany?"

"We could fly to England and support the Allies in the Second World War. We would be a big help with our technology."

"If we want to shorten the Second World War, then we might as well also let Hitler die. We would be in the same situation as now. The war would be over before the atom bombs are tested," Christoph snapped.

"Yes, yes, you're right of course," Reuter said. "We mustn't change the course of history again. Who knows what the consequences would be."

"The safest thing to do would be to prevent the assassination and then disappear completely."

Reuter looked at him askance. "What do you want to do? Crash the Airbus into the sea? Commit suicide?"

"I don't know, damn it!" Christoph closed his eyes, feeling exhausted.

"We could stay in 1939 for just a short time, prevent the assassination and fly back to the Eifel through the wormhole. Once we've straightened out the events of history again, we should come out in our own present day again."

Christoph thought hard. Could it work? The truth was, he didn't know. The whole thing was too much for his brain to process. "Even if we prevent the assassination, we've still changed the course of history. Would we still come out in our own present, the way we know it?"

"We need to align the course of history as closely as possible to the history we know," Reuter said emphatically. "It's our only chance."

Christoph shrugged in resignation. He was just the pilot, and shouldn't have to make these kinds of decisions. But what other choice did they have?

"OK. Let's give it a go." He looked over at Steinmann, who was still kneeling in front of his wife's grave. "What do we do with him?"

Reuter ran a hand through his hair. "I'm not sure whether we should take him with us. It might lead to a time paradox ..."

"Spare me your time paradoxes," Christoph said sharply. "We are not going to leave him here to die."

Reuter shrugged. "What the hell. Surely one life won't make a difference." He sighed. "Do you want to tell him the truth or shall I?"

29

"My God, this plane is huge," Steinmann looked awestruck as they approached the glassy runway of the former Cologne Airport. The wild grass of Wahn Heath was covered in hoarfrost. The sun had already risen quite far over the eastern horizon, but at this time of year it didn't have enough strength to warm up the air quickly.

Steinmann stopped the vehicle next to the runway. The wing of the A380 towered over them. Christoph saw Patrick running down the emergency stairs. He gave him a sign not to come up to them yet. First they had to talk to Steinmann.

He clambered out of the back seat and helped the old man out of the car. "Come with me, we'll take a walk around the plane."

"I remember the plans of the Hughes aircraft company. They wanted to construct a two-story plane. That was in the sixties, shortly before the world went to hell. I wouldn't have thought there was anywhere left in the world where a plan like that could still be carried out." Steinmann's voice was full of wonder.

They approached the back of the plane. Christoph's mind was racing. How could he tell this man the truth without giving him too much of a shock? Reuter, trudging along gloomily behind them, probably wouldn't be much help.

Steinmann stopped under the tail and shook his head. "There's the flag of the Weimar Republic again. Did you buy the plane from the Americans?" He turned to face Christoph and gave him an inquisitive look. "Where are your headquarters? And why have you only come now? I answered all of your questions. Now I'd like some answers from you."

Christoph nodded. "Yes, that's only fair." He pointed at the German flag. "What would you say if I told you we haven't come from the USA?"

"Then I'm guessing you've come from somewhere in the southern hemisphere. Argentina, perhaps? There were several immigrant colonies there. Or South Africa? Namibia?"

Christoph shook his head. "I grew up in Germany."

"You mean the German Reich?" Steinmann asked in confusion.

"I mean in Germany. To be precise in the Federal Republic of Germany."

"And where, may I ask, is that?"

Christoph took a deep breath. "The Germany in which I was born, and for the most part grew up in, emerged out of the German Reich, which due to Adolf Hitler was responsible for the deaths of millions of people in a war called the Second World War. We were defeated by the Allies in 1945 after Hitler committed suicide in Berlin."

"Hitler died in 1939 in the attack in Munich," Steinmann laughed in confusion.

"In the world in which I grew up, the assassination attempt took place, but it failed, because Elser had set the timer a quarter of an hour too late."

"What are you talking about?"

"After the Second World War there was also an arms race between various power blocs, but that ended in the nineties, thankfully without a nuclear war. The nuclear weapons were tested in Japan in 1945 and two cities—Hiroshima and Nagasaki—were razed to the ground. The images of what happened there served as a warning to never let it happen again. Germany experienced an unprecedented economic boom after the war and together with other European countries became part of the European Union, a peaceful federation of member states."

Steinmann pursed his lips.

Christoph could see the man didn't believe him. But he continued, all the same. "Scientific and technological progress followed. That included the development of this aircraft, which was jointly produced by the European states. Very recently, an incredible discovery was made: how to travel in time and explore the past."

"Are you seriously trying to tell me you've come from the future?" Steinmann's voice was full of contempt.

"No, we haven't come from the future," Reuter interrupted. "We have come from the present. We made our journey in this plane, which has a time machine on board. Originally we wanted to go back only a day into the past, to study the nature of time. You see that man there?" He pointed at Werner, who was standing on the steps next to Patrick. Steinmann turned around to look.

"That man hijacked the plane, took it back to 1939 and made sure the assassination on Hitler was successful," Christoph said. "When we returned to the present, this is the world we found. Destroyed by a global nuclear war."

Steinmann's eyes moved back and forth between Christoph and Reuter. His face was expressionless. He turned around and walked a few paces away from the plane. Then he looked at Christoph again. "What are you talking about? Why are you telling me fairy tales? Why can't you simply tell me where you've come from?"

Christoph didn't know what to answer. Reuter remained silent, too.

"What made you think I would believe a story like that?"

"Because it's the truth," Christoph said quietly. "You said it yourself: the world has been destroyed. There are probably just a few people left scattered around the planet waiting for the end. There is nowhere on Earth left that an aircraft like this could be built. You also noticed that we are well nourished."

"True—I didn't think that would be possible anywhere anymore. But traveling through time? Sorry, that's completely unbelievable!" Steinmann chuckled softly.

Christoph reached into the breast pocket of his overalls and fished out his cell phone. He activated it.

"What's that?" Steinmann asked mistrustfully.

"We call it a smartphone. It's a bit like a personal computer."

He tapped on the display and opened his photo album. He swiped a few pictures aside and stood next to Steinmann, so that he could see the screen.

"What's that?" Steinmann asked again.

"It's Cologne Cathedral."

"It no longer exists!" Steinmann said. Now there was a hint of uncertainty in his voice.

Christoph scrolled on and showed Steinmann pictures of Cologne that he had taken in the city center the week before. "And this is Cologne Airport. You can see all the people on the apron, and our plane in the background. That was about two weeks ago."

Steinmann stared at Christoph. He opened his mouth to speak but no words came out. He looked at the Airbus and then back at Christoph. "You're telling the truth?" he whispered.

Christoph nodded. "We set off less than twenty-four hours ago."

Steinmann didn't say anything for several long seconds, then shook his head. "I don't understand. I mean, you're telling me you set off from a utopian Germany. You flew your funny time machine to 1939, killed Hitler and came back to this changed present? And all that in less than twenty-four hours?"

Christoph knew how ridiculous it sounded. He nodded.

"That's impossible," Steinmann said. "I've spent my whole life here. I've lived through everything that happened since 1939. The upheavals of the German Reich in my childhood, which—my God—weren't easy. I went to university, married my wife. Then the nuclear war and the fifty years we spent in the bunker." He no longer sounded skeptical but furious. His voice grew louder. "My whole life, everything I've seen, felt, thought, was decided by one fateful day in 1939? I can assure you: this life is not an illusion that you have conjured up in the last twenty-four hours."

Christoph didn't know what to answer. Reuter stepped forward and tried to reassure Steinmann. "It was never our intention to change the past. We were forced to do it by Werner and his accomplice. That's why we intend to return to 1939 and undo the change we made to history."

Steinmann laughed. A despairing laugh. "So you want to change the change? Do you know how absurd that sounds? I don't even know about any first change. From my point of view, you're setting out to destroy my past. And what happens then? Will I cease to exist? Will I never have met my wife? Will the ruins of my present turn into the skyscrapers of a utopian world? I'm not saying this world and my life are particularly pleasant, but still, it is my life and I have had experiences I'm glad about."

"Our intention was to find out something about the nature of time," Reuter explained calmly. "We did not want to trigger such drastic changes. We would like to invite you to accompany us."

Steinmann didn't respond for a while. "I don't know," he said slowly. "This is my present. My world and my history. What would happen if I just stayed here and you're successful in your mission? Will I suddenly change into a Mr. Steinmann with a completely different history? A history in which I might be rich and successful and have forgotten everything about my time in a nuclear bunker?" He stared intently at Reuter.

"I don't know," Reuter admitted. "We don't know enough about the nature of time to say for sure."

"You can decide whether you want to join us or not," Christoph said. "But what else awaits you here except death? You have nothing to lose."

"Apart from my entire existence!" Steinmann countered bitterly.

"We have to go," Reuter said after looking at his watch. "Otherwise we'll be too late to save Hitler."

Christoph closed his eyes for a moment.

... to save Hitler!

30

"The engines look good," Christoph said, his eyes on the display. "We're ready for departure."

He was hoping that Patrick, who was sitting beside him, could help him a little. They had locked Werner in the toilet again. Although he had meekly insisted that he would do everything to help restore the original course of history, Christoph didn't trust him. Reuter was sitting behind him at his console. As the capacitors had run out of power, they no longer had the time machine at their disposal, but at least he had access to the monitoring tools, which might be helpful. And he could use the console to stay in contact with his team at the back of the plane. Beside him sat Steinmann, who in the end had decided to accompany them.

"All clear from my side, too. We can start," Reuter confirmed.

"Good." Christoph pushed the thrust lever forward a little and released the parking brake. The plane jolted into motion. Using the tiller, Christoph maneuvered the plane so they were facing the end of the runway. There was no wind, so they wouldn't have a problem starting in a south-easterly direction. He checked the instruments a final time. "Looks good. We have twenty-one minutes until we reach the wormhole over the Eifel. Are you sure the wormhole mouth will still be in exactly the same position?"

"Absolutely sure. That much we were able to prove in lab tests," Reuter said decisively.

"If it's moved by even a few feet, we could tear off one of the wings when we fly through."

"Don't worry! The wormhole remains stable and

doesn't move until it collapses. On the other side, just as much time should have passed as here, about twenty hours, so it will be about half past five in the afternoon. That gives us around four hours to make radio contact with the government and prevent the assassination. That ought to be more than enough time."

Christoph sighed and moved the thrust levers forward. The plane gathered speed as it shot along the asphalt. It juddered more than Christoph was used to, but it wasn't difficult to keep the Airbus in the middle of the runway. He would have liked to have a competent first officer at his side, but on this occasion he would have to manage alone. A few seconds later, they were in the air. Christoph pushed up the landing gear lever and pulled in the flaps. Then he activated the autopilot and set the aircraft on a south-westerly course.

He took one last look out the right-hand cockpit window and saw the foundations and glassy streets of what had once been Bonn. He wondered if they would succeed in restoring the old course of time. Whatever they did, it couldn't be worse than the world they were flying away from.

He changed the scale of the navigation display using the control knob. A red circle marked the location of the wormhole mouth. Christoph adjusted the course slightly so that they would fly straight through it. "Fifteen minutes to go."

"Who are we going to contact by radio?" Patrick asked.

"What?"

"We wanted to warn the Nazis by radio. Do we even have a frequency on which we can make direct contact to some high-ranking official?"

"Unfortunately not," Christoph said. "I'll just go through all the frequencies until I get an answer from someone and then ask to be connected."

"And you think they'll believe us? Who do we say we are?"

"All they have to do is take a look in the damn column behind Hitler's ass. Then they'll find the bomb," Reuter said.

Hopefully it's really that easy, Christoph thought. He checked the navigation display again and adjusted the altitude. In a few minutes, they would know.

Steinmann sat quietly in his seat. He hadn't said a word since they had taken off. Christoph couldn't tell how the old man was feeling. What must it be like to find out your whole life was an illusion, the result of a mishap in a journey through time? What would happen if they were successful and managed to hinder the assassination? Would Steinmann dissolve into thin air? Disappear together with the changed timeline? Christoph couldn't believe it would be that simple.

A signal sounded through the cockpit. The onboard computer indicated that they were about to enter the wormhole. Just three more miles. Christoph reduced speed slightly and double-checked that they were on exactly the right course and flying at the right altitude. The indicator glowed green. They would fly right through the center of the wormhole mouth.

"I can't see anything," Christoph said quietly, leaning over the instrument console. "From everything I've seen in science-fiction movies, I expected to see a funnel or some kind of visual effect. But there's really nothing."

"I also expected some kind of visual distortion,"

Reuter replied. "It seems the light is diffracted differently from the way we calculated it."

"It's straight ahead," Christoph said. "Another two and a half miles. Get ready."

"I hope it's still there," Patrick muttered.

Nobody answered him.

The autopilot kept the plane on a steady course headed for the center of the wormhole. As the small cross on the navigation display neared the red circle, Christoph' clenched the edge of his seat. "Four, three, two, one ..."

Suddenly the quality of the light changed. The sun, which a moment ago had come from the front, was now shining into the side of the cockpit. No jolt, no sound, not even the slightest vibration. But they had passed through the mouth of the wormhole.

"Incredible," Reuter whispered. "Just as predicted. We should have enough time to warn Hitler."

"Yes, I'm changing to a south-easterly course." Something was nagging at Christoph, but right now he didn't have time to think about it.

"Are we really in 1939?" Steinmann asked.

"Yes. It's November 8, 1939, to be precise. The day of Hitler's assassination," Reuter said.

Steinmann looked awestruck but didn't respond.

Christoph forced the plane into a long left turn toward Munich. Slowly the cockpit passed into shadow and the sun popped up in the left-hand window, blinding Christoph.

The left-hand window? Now Christoph knew what was bothering him. If it was really late afternoon, and they were on a southerly course, the sun should be on their right. Or hadn't they come out of the wormhole in a southerly direction?

Christoph looked to the left and saw the Rhine some distance away. They were definitely heading south!

"We might have a problem," he said out loud.

"What do you mean?" Reuter asked.

"According to the position of the sun, it isn't afternoon, but morning."

"That can't be," Reuter insisted.

"Go see for yourself!"

Reuter unbuckled himself and stood up to look out of the window. "Are you sure we're flying south?"

"Absolutely. There's the Rhine."

Reuter's eyes followed Christoph's outstretched finger. "Hmm, yes. But why?" he whispered.

"It must mean that wormhole mouths don't move in parallel through time," Patrick said.

"But my calculations ..."

"To hell with your calculations," Christoph couldn't control himself. "You were wrong! The big question now is whether time here has passed slower or faster. If it's passed more slowly, then it's still November 8th, but in the morning. If it's passed more quickly ..."

"... then it's already the 9th," Patrick whispered.

"We need to find out, and quick. Turn on the radio!"

Reuter went back to his console and activated the surveillance instruments. It took only a few seconds until he tuned into a radio program. A crackly but comprehensible male voice echoed through the cockpit. "... is still unclear. Reich Minister Göring said he is sure that British agents are behind the attack. Revenge will be wreaked and the death of the Führer ..."

Reuter switched the radio off. He had turned pale. "Hitler is dead. We're too late!"

Nobody said a word. Christoph looked out of the window. In front of him he could already see the lowlands of the Rhine-Main region. It made no sense to fly on to Munich. He steered the plane into a left curve again. They would circle over the foothills of the Hunsrück until they had decided what to do next.

But what other options did they have?

"Your plan has failed," Steinmann said slowly. "Let's return through the wormhole to the present."

"And then?" Patrick asked. "Wait to die in that post-apocalyptic world?"

"We could fly as far south as possible until we come across other people, and join them," Steinmann suggested.

"You said yourself," Christoph retorted, "that it's nothing more than a rumor that there are survivors in the Mediterranean. Everybody there might be dead, too. And we don't have enough fuel to fly any further."

"Couldn't we simply stay here?" Patrick suggested.

"What?" Reuter snapped. "Here in the Third Reich? We're responsible for Hitler's death, remember? They would lynch us as soon as we landed."

"We could fly to the Allies. To England. And warn people there of the impending nuclear disaster."

Reuter snorted. "There have always been warnings about the dangers of a nuclear war. And anyway: us with our twenty-first-century technology at the beginning of the 1940s? Who knows what kind of time paradox that would trigger?"

"It could hardly be worse than the world we just

left behind!" Patrick cried.

"We can't stay here," Christoph intervened in a calm voice. "Even if we wanted to."

"And why not?" Reuter asked.

"We need a runway that's at least two miles long for the Airbus. As far as I know, no such thing existed in Europe at the time."

"Shit! Can't we attempt an emergency landing somewhere?" Patrick asked.

Christoph shook his head. "Not a good idea."

"Somewhere where?" Reuter asked Patrick.

"On water. Just off the coast, for example."

"That would be dangerous," Christoph said. "The plane could be ripped apart on the waves."

"But that guy in New York managed it."

"He landed on the Hudson. A calm river without any waves. And it was a much smaller plane. We could try it on a big river like the Elbe, but it would be a game of Russian roulette.

"So our only other choice is to fly back through the wormhole," Reuter whispered.

"Unfortunately, yes," Christoph said. It wasn't a pleasant prospect. They would have to come to terms with spending the rest of their lives in a dying world. And they would have to live with the fact that they had caused the downfall of humanity by meddling with the course of history. Maybe it really would be better to risk an emergency landing. If it failed, they would die. If they survived, they still had a small chance of averting disaster. They would create a new time paradox and a new history for the period of 1939, but, as Patrick had pointed out, it couldn't get any worse. Silently, Christoph cursed the scientists who had built this damn time machine. "We could try the Thames," he said finally.

"The Thames?" Reuter asked in disbelief.

Christoph nodded. "Just outside London the river is calm enough to attempt an emergency landing."

"Didn't you just say it was like a game of Russian roulette?" Reuter sounded irritated.

"Yes," Christoph answered angrily. "But what's our alternative? Return to the present?"

Reuter shut his mouth.

"Isn't there an airport near London where we could land?" Patrick asked.

"The main airport in London until World War II was Croydon Airport. I don't know how long the runway was, but I'm sure it was no longer than a half a mile. No, we can't land there."

"Shit," Patrick buried his head in his hands.

"And why not fly back to the present and search for some sign of life in the Mediterranean?" Reuter suggested. "Then we might be able to charge the capacitors."

"And then?" Christoph asked.

"Return back to the time before the assassination and maybe prevent it after all."

"That's pure speculation. If there's nothing left there, we're stuck. That is, if we even find somewhere to land," Patrick said.

Christoph nodded. "We still have enough fuel for two hours' flight. We could just reach the north of Spain or Italy. Then we'd have to land immediately, we wouldn't have much leeway."

"If there are any people left alive, they must be further south," Steinmann said. "I know that Catalonia in Spain was destroyed, as well as the cities of northern Italy. We would need to get as far as

Sicily or Andalusia."

"We don't have enough fuel for that," Christoph said.

"So that leaves the Thames," Patrick concluded.

"I still think it's a crazy idea. If we land on the Thames, we'll never be able to get the plane back up in the air. It will be the end of any chance of going back in time again," Reuter said.

"I'm for the Thames," Patrick said firmly.

Christoph nodded. "Me too. We simply can't make it to southern Europe. I'm sorry."

"I say we should risk going to the present!" Reuter insisted.

"Our only chance is the Thames," Christoph said. But he was doubtful himself. What if he was mistaken? Their final opportunity to restore the original timeline would be gone. Both options could cost them their lives. And what were the chances of averting a nuclear war even if they did make a successful landing? Could there be a third option? Something none of them had thought of yet? They didn't have enough time to discuss it. With every second that they circled over the Taunus mountains, they were losing more fuel. They had to make a decision. *He* had to make a decision!

Christoph breathed deeply in and out. Then he adjusted the autopilot.

"What are you doing?" Reuter asked.

"I'm changing to a northerly course."

"We haven't made a decision yet!" Reuter cried in a shrill voice.

"I'm making one now," Christoph replied calmly.

"What gives you the right ...?" Reuter choked on his words. "I repeat: We haven't made a decision."

Christoph pointed at the display. "See this? We're using up four liters of kerosene per second. We can't afford to wait any longer. I have made a decision. We have enough fuel for two more hours. That isn't enough time to fly through the wormhole and down to the Mediterranean, where we would first have to look for somewhere to land. If we don't find an intact airport right away, we would have to land on the open sea, and our chances of survival would be less than slim. For a water landing, the Thames is the best option, unless we choose the Elbe."

"And what were the criteria for your decision?" Reuter shouted. "The safety of the crew?"

Christoph shook his head. "No. Then we have to fly back through the wormhole and land in Cologne. That's the only place we know for sure we can land. Would you prefer I do that?"

"There's nothing left in Cologne!"

Christoph looked out of the cockpit window. The plane had completed the curve and was flying north. The Rhine was now to their right. They had already left the wormhole behind them.

Christoph turned back to Reuter. "Give me a valid alternative!"

"This is about saving the future!" Reuter screamed. He jumped up from his seat. "We have to find a way of landing in the present and charging the capacitors, so that we can undo the mess that Werner has created."

"Don't you get it?" Christoph asked calmly. "We don't have that option. Accept the reality."

Reuter sat down again. "I get that you're responsible for the plane and the crew." He glared at Christoph. "I hope you're also aware of the implications of your decision. The fate of humanity is now in your hands. Are you prepared to take on that responsibility?"

The fate of humanity ... really? Could one man possibly take on a responsibility of such magnitude? No, he hadn't led the world into a nuclear war. And unlike Werner, he hadn't wanted to change history. He was only responsible for the aircraft and its occupants—and could only make a decision on that basis.

Christoph looked down on Cologne—the Cologne of 1939, its historic city center still intact, before it was devastated by air raids in the Second World War.

What should he do? Fly to the Thames? Listen to Reuter? Look for an airport here, where they might be able to charge the capacitors? He didn't want to make the decision. He didn't want to carry this weight of responsibility. And yet he was in charge of this plane and had to decide where to fly it.

Two hours' worth of fuel. They would need an hour to reach London. Two or three approaches to land as gently as possible on the water ... another half hour. They didn't have much leeway.

"We'll stay on a northerly course," he said. "We'll reach the North Sea in about half an hour. Until then we can still consider alternatives. Then I will start to prepare the plane for a water landing."

"Why a northerly course?" Patrick asked. "The most direct route would be via Belgium."

"Germany is at war, and even if it isn't fighting the Benelux countries, I don't want to cross the German border. That's why we'll fly out over the North Sea, and then turn left toward England."

"But we *are* at war with England," Reuter said.

"And they already have a radar system. They'll send fighter planes and shoot us down, especially if we head straight for London."

"I don't like it either," Christoph admitted. "But I also don't like any of the alternatives. The Thames is still the best option."

"Perhaps I should have stayed at home," Steinmann sighed.

"And starved to death?" Reuter answered drily.

"I guess you're right."

"If we fly over the North Sea, we'll be back near the old wormhole," Patrick pointed out.

"That doesn't help us," Reuter snapped. "For one thing, we wouldn't find it anymore, because the memory of the inertial navigation has been erased, and for another it doesn't make a difference which hole we fly through. Hitler is dead. We didn't manage to restore the old course of time."

"What would have happened if you'd succeeded?" Steinmann asked. "We would have returned to a changed present. Changed for me at least. Would I have been replaced by another version of myself or would I have landed with you in a utopian Cologne and gone in search of myself?"

"I don't know," Reuter said and turned back to his console.

Christoph looked at Steinmann thoughtfully. It was an interesting question. Could a person exist twice at the same point in time? Just thinking about it made his head spin—and gave him the feeling they had overlooked something important.

"What if we land here and now," he said to Reuter. "I mean, Steinmann was born in September 1939. He could simply go to his parents' house and see himself in his cradle."

"Well, yes, maybe, but how does that help us?"

"And what about us?" Christoph continued. "When Werner changed the past, we also didn't just disappear. We returned to the changed present. If everybody hadn't died in the nuclear war, we would have been able to visit ourselves too ... I mean, our counterparts, who grew up in that world."

"I don't know," Reuter shrugged.

"For Christ's sake!" Patrick screamed at his boss. "You're the expert!"

Reuter winced and hunched up in his seat.

"And if we had saved Hitler and then returned to the present?" Christoph continued his train of thought. "That would also have been a different history. Then, too, we could have met our counterparts when we returned, the ones who had grown up during that time, right?"

"What are you getting at?" Patrick asked.

"Could it be that every time we make a change, we create a new version of history, but the old one continues to exist?"

"A kind of changed copy of history? It doesn't sound very credible," Patrick said skeptically.

"Yes, but everything we've experienced suggests that's what happens." Christoph nodded at Steinmann: "He comes from another version of history than ours. Another universe, if you like. And yet we're sitting here in the cockpit together."

"Well, I still don't get ..." Patrick trailed off.

"The wormholes!" Christoph cried out, more and more convinced by his hypothesis. It was the only solution that made any sense. "The wormholes don't just connect different *times*, they connect different *universes.* We created the last wormhole *after* we had changed the course of history. That's why it led to this apocalyptic future."

"And the first ... wormhole?" Steinmann asked, who had never heard the term before today.

"It was created *before* we altered the course of history. So it ought to take us back to our own world, where we set out from." Christoph turned around in his seat. "Reuter?"

"The Everett hypothesis," he replied slowly.

"What?"

"Hugh Everett was a quantum physicist. He believed that in the case of certain quantum effects, the universe splits and different versions of it exist side by side."

Christoph could hardly believe his ears. "You ... you knew about it?"

Reuter shook his head. "I rejected the parallel world hypothesis. I believed in the Copenhagen interpretation."

"*Believed?*" Christoph scoffed. He would have liked to grab Reuter by the throat. "I thought you were a scientist! I always assumed people in your profession either know or don't know."

"In some areas there are different interpretations of accepted theories," Reuter replied brusquely. "And it's common for different factions ..."

"But you knew the hypothesis and didn't even *consider* it?" Christoph turned to Patrick. "Did you know about it?"

He shook his head. "I've never had anything to do with quantum physics. I'm an engineer, not a scientist. I also don't really get—"

Christoph turned back to Reuter. "So you're saying

there's a fair chance we'll come out in our present again if we fly through the old wormhole."

"No!" Reuter flared up. "I don't think so, because I don't believe in the theory."

"But there are other scientists who *would* believe it."

"Yes, and they're idiots!"

"It looks like our only real chance of getting back home. Maybe it was all along!" Christoph said firmly.

"And even if it is," Reuter said coolly. "We'll never find it. The navigation memory ... remember?"

"Damn it," Christoph closed his eyes. If Reuter wasn't so narrow-minded and had thought about this possibility earlier, then they could have worked out a way of maybe finding the wormhole again. But now? In the distance he could already see the rippled surface of the North Sea. Somewhere out there was the wormhole, and maybe a way back home.

31

"We need to get through that wormhole!" Christoph said. "Think! How can we find it?" He adjusted the course on the autopilot, and the plane began to turn slightly to the right. "We have about fifteen minutes left to find an answer."

"Impossible," Reuter said. "We'll never find it."

"Why not?"

"Because the wormhole mouth bends the light around it. We talked about it already. Only mass can pass through it. That's why we can't see it."

"Does it maybe have a magnetic field we could detect with our compass? Emit radiation that could be detected with sensors?"

"No."

"What kind of sensors do we have?" Patrick asked and turned in his seat to look at Reuter.

Reuter shrugged. "Optical cameras, radiometers, and the infrared camera."

Patrick turned around again and folded his arms across his chest.

"What is infrared?" Steinmann asked. "I've heard of it, but I never understood it."

"It's just light in a different wavelength range," Christoph explained.

"It's used above all to detect thermal radiation. That's why it's used in thermal imaging cameras," Reuter added.

Christoph' ears perked up. "Heat, Reuter!" he cried. "You said only mass could pass through the wormhole?"

"Yes."

"Wind, too?"

"What?"

"Can air penetrate the wormhole?"

Reuter wavered, then nodded. "Yes, I think so. After all, there are pressure differences so that an exchange of air ..." His eyes widened. "I see what you're getting at!"

"Me too," Patrick said. He shifted excitedly back and forth in his seat. "Maybe we can see the wormhole with the infrared camera."

"Do you think so?" Christoph asked.

"Yes," Reuter replied. "If air penetrates or flows out from the wormhole from the other side, it will change the temperature of the area around the wormhole. We should be able to see that on the screen." He groaned. "I can't believe we didn't think of it before."

"Will the wormhole still *be* there?" Christoph asked.

Reuter looked at his watch. "Thirty-six hours. If it is, then not for much longer." He looked directly at Christoph. "I can't say for sure."

"Let's hope for the best," Christoph mumbled, and tapped a new command into the onboard computer. "And let's hope we really find it."

A few miles ahead of them, the shoreline came into view. In a few minutes they would fly through the airspace between the islands of Langeoog and Spiekeroog. To their left were the islands of Baltrum, Nordeney, and Juist. Visibility was perfect. They would pass Helgoland to the west.

"Do you really think this wormhole will take us back to your present and not mine?" Steinmann asked.

"I don't think so," Reuter answered.

"I don't know," Patrick said.

But Christoph was convinced. It was the only way of explaining why they hadn't all disappeared after the change was made in 1939. He looked at Steinmann. "I think so." Or was it just wishful thinking? If they were going to find out, they had to first find the damn wormhole.

Christoph looked at the navigation display and out of the window again. They were leaving the coast behind them and flying over the tidal flats. He wanted to make another turn when something flashed in the corner of his eye. A light reflex? He closed his eyes and scanned the shoreline. There! A small, bright spot was moving toward them from below. And beside it, another one. And another. It could only mean one thing!

Reuter had noticed the startled look on Christoph's face. "What is it?"

"They've found us," Christoph said in a hoarse voice. "There are four planes heading our way. Quick."

32

"Planes? What ...?" Reuter stammered.

Patrick leaned forward. "Where?"

Christoph pointed out of the window. "To our left and below us. Fighter aircraft."

"So they *did* have a radar system in 1939," Patrick said quietly.

Christoph laughed bitterly. "Visibility is fantastic and we're flying very low. They don't need a radar to spot us."

The squadron had almost reached them. Two of the aircraft broke off to the right and a few seconds later disappeared from Christoph's line of sight. The other aircraft flew up to the same height as the A380 and approached from behind. They were propeller aircraft—the kind Christoph knew from old films and museums. The red flag with the swastika in a white circle was clearly visible on their tails.

"Two of the planes are right next to us. I can see the faces of the pilots in their cockpits," Christoph said.

"The other two are on our right," Patrick said nervously. "What are they going to do?"

Christoph looked into the cockpit of one of the planes flying next to them. The face of the pilot stood out as a bright circle behind the glass. It was impossible to see his eyes. Christoph couldn't imagine what was going on in the man's mind at the sight of this huge A380. "I don't think they know themselves. The question is: How long will their surprise last and what will they do then?"

"What kind of aircraft are they?" Reuter asked, who couldn't see the planes from his console.

"I think they're Messerschmitts. Bf 109. The standard fighter planes of the time. I've seen them in museums."

"But they're propeller planes?"

"Yes."

"So how can they fly as fast as us?"

"Powerful propeller aircraft could reach almost the speed of sound. Although not these early versions. We're flying low, and because of the time machine we're also very heavy, that's why we're flying relatively slowly. Two hundred and fifty knots doesn't seem to be a problem for them."

Christoph looked at the navigation display again. They had passed the East Frisian Islands and were flying out into the North Sea. Another sixty miles until they reached the wormhole.

"They're leaving!" Patrick cried.

Christoph looked to the left. The planes were dropping back without losing height. His heart skipped a beat. "No! They're positioning themselves behind us!"

"To do what?" Reuter asked, panic creeping into his voice.

"To fire at us!" Christoph pushed the lever on the center console all the way forward. The engines roared. He waited a few seconds before switching off the autopilot and pulled the sidestick. The horizon disappeared below the window.

"What are you doing?" Steinmann screamed.

"Going up!" Christoph shouted. "The fighter planes can obviously keep up with our speed but I don't think the early versions of the Bf 109 could fly very high."

Eighteen thousand feet. They were climbing fast,

but losing speed in the process. Christoph looked out of the window. He couldn't see the Messerschmitts. But they might still be behind them.

"What's that?" Patrick cried.

Sparks were flying past the aircraft.

"Tracer ammunition! They're firing!" Christoph pulled the sidestick to the right. The plane went into a wide left curve, immediately slowing their ascent. Christoph took them out of the curve.

A sound like hail on a corrugated roof droned through the cockpit. They'd been hit!

Reuter shot up out of his seat. "Why are they firing? We didn't do anything!"

"Hitler was killed yesterday," Christoph replied. "They will have been instructed to shoot first and ask questions later."

Twenty thousand feet. They were ascending too slowly! More sparks flew past them. Christoph pulled the sidestick to the left again, this time more cautiously.

"Can't this tin can go up any faster?" Patrick sounded frantic. He was gripping the side of his seat so hard his knuckles had turned white.

"We're too heavy," Christoph said. A warning sound wailed through the cockpit. "We're losing pressure! They must have hit the cabin!"

"Have we been badly hit?" Patrick wanted to know.

"No, thank God. The pressure is dropping very slowly."

Twenty-five thousand feet.

They were climbing even more slowly. With their weight they wouldn't make it any higher than thirty thousand. Hopefully that would be enough!

"Reuter! Check if everything is OK out back!"

"Roger," Reuter answered, white as a sheet.

The sparks had stopped. "I think they've gone," Patrick said, staring out of the window.

Thirty thousand feet. Christoph angled the plane so they were facing the horizon again, and it began to pick up speed. He hoped they were high enough to have escaped the fighter planes. He activated the autopilot and got the plane back on course for the wormhole.

"Everything is OK in the back," Reuter reported. "But they're scared!"

"Then explain what happened and what we're planning to do. We seem to have shaken off the fighters."

Christoph was relieved that the shots hadn't damaged any vital systems. He didn't want to imagine what would have happened if they'd hit one of the fuel tanks!

"We're nearing the test area. The wormhole must be somewhere in front of us. Switch on the infrared sensors," he commanded Reuter. In front of them they could see the wide expanse of the North Sea.

"I've switched it on," Reuter confirmed. "But the camera's field of vision is limited. I don't know where to look."

Christoph changed the scale of the navigation display. He typed the approximate coordinates of the wormhole into the onboard computer and turned back to the screens. The line ended a few miles to the left in front of them. He forced the plane into a slight left turn so that they were circling the area in a wide radius. They were now flying at thirty thousand feet, while the wormhole was at a height of about sixteen thousand feet. It must be somewhere below them. "Point the camera to the left. About eighty degrees, with a forty-five degree gradient."

Reuter cursed as he adjusted the settings on his console. "I can't see anything."

"Maybe it's already collapsed," Patrick said.

"Then our only option is the Thames." Christoph looked at the fuel gauge. "We have ten minutes to find it, then we'll have to stop the search."

Slowly the Airbus completed its curve and they were back on a southerly course. In the distance Christoph could see the North Sea coast and the East Frisian Islands. There was nothing to be seen of the fighter planes. It looks like they had returned to their bases.

"I can't find anything!" Reuter said. "At least not in the area you told me to look."

Seven more minutes.

"Then swing the camera around a bit."

"The controls are very stiff," Reuter groaned, and wiped the sweat from his brow.

The minutes passed quickly. They flew another wide curve and then another. Christoph had to force himself not to look out of the window the whole time—the wormhole wasn't visible to the naked eye.

The ten minutes were up. "Now what?"

"Nothing," Reuter answered, resigned. "I don't see anything. Maybe the wormhole really did collapse already."

So that was it—their last hope was gone. "OK," Christoph said quietly. "I'm going to take a westerly course."

"Wait!" Reuter shouted. "I see something!"

Christoph spun round.

His boss was pointing at the screen in front of him. Christoph couldn't see the screen from where he was sitting. "I think the contrast was too low, hold on." Reuter turned a knob, closed his eyes and nodded. Then he turned back to Christoph and smiled tentatively. "I've found an anomaly. In one small area the temperature is slightly higher than the air around it. That must be the wormhole."

"Give it to me!" Christoph switched one of the monitors to AUX 2.

He could see it. Reuter was right. The screen was blue. But on the right-hand edge was a circular area with a reddish glow.

"I didn't think we'd find it this way," Reuter whispered.

"And now what?" Patrick wanted to know.

"Now we're going to fly in a big curve, drop our altitude and fly through it," Christoph said firmly.

"And then we're home?"

"I still can't believe it," Reuter frowned.

"We'll soon see." Christoph began to turn the plane after he'd marked the spot with the help of the onboard computer. "I'm reducing our altitude," he explained and was about to set the autopilot when Patrick screamed.

"Don't!"

"What is it?"

"There!" Patrick pointed outside. "Those planes again!"

"You're right!" Below them were four Messerschmitts. They were circling over the spot where the wormhole must be. If he flew on course, he would be flying straight toward them.

"Shit! As soon as we go lower, they'll get us."

"Why are they back?" Reuter asked.

"They probably followed us at a distance and noticed we were circling. They're just waiting for us to come back down."

"And now what?" Reuter asked.

Christoph didn't have an answer. What could he do? Should he continue the approach as planned and hope they weren't hit too badly? No, that made no sense, the Airbus was too big a target. He had to think of something. Time was running out!

"I said, what now?" Reuter's voice sounded hysterical.

"Calm down!" Christoph remembered a situation he'd practiced in a simulator not long ago. He had to descend to the wormhole as quickly as possible. He didn't know if it would work, but it was their only chance.

"Make sure you're strapped in! And point the infrared camera forward at a forty-five degree angle," he instructed Reuter. "And Patrick—tell everyone at the back to buckle up."

"What are you planning to do?"

"Emergency descent!"

Christoph flew in a tight curve until the plane was aimed directly at the wormhole. It was three miles in front of them and two and a half miles below them. He could see the reddish circle flickering on his screen.

"Let's go!" He pulled the thrust levers all the way back, until the engines were in idle. Then he pulled the speed brake all the way back, too.

Immediately, the Airbus began to go down. The whole aircraft vibrated.

"We're going to crash!" Reuter screamed.

Christoph ignored him. He pushed the sidestick forward. It wasn't going to be a precision flight. The red area on the monitor wandered to the right and Christoph steered toward it. How was he going to get through the wormhole with all this vibration?

"This is never going to work!" Patrick screamed. "We'll only fly half the plane through the hole, and tear off the wings!"

They were falling like a stone from the sky. They were already at twenty-three thousand feet. Christoph desperately tried to keep the aircraft on course.

Reuter retched loudly and threw up on the floor.

"They're firing again!" Patrick shouted.

Christoph had no time to look out of the window. He was struggling to keep on course with the help of the screen.

Again he heard that eerie sound. Like hail on a car roof. Don't think about it, he told himself.

Eighteen thousand feet. The red circle on the screen was getting bigger and bigger. The wormhole must be right in front of them! A jolt shook the plane as they were hit by turbulence. That's all they needed!

Sweat was running into Christoph's eyes. The screen was a deep red. Fifteen thousand feet!

Suddenly it was dark in the cockpit.

They were through!

33

"We've gone through the wormhole!" Christoph cried in relief. He glanced at the system display. No warning lights, no damage. They had flown straight through and hadn't torn off a wing. But the plane was still sinking like a stone toward the surface of the water.

Christoph rammed the speed brake lever forward and gave the engines full thrust.

Ten thousand feet. They were still going down.

He pulled the sidestick gently, but the heavy aircraft only started to rise very slowly.

Eight thousand feet.

"Get this plane under control!" Reuter screeched.

Seven thousand feet.

Had they been hit by one of the fighter planes after all? The Airbus normally didn't react this sluggishly. Christoph had to be careful not to put too much G-Force on the aircraft.

Then, finally, the engines had built up enough thrust. They picked up speed.

Five thousand feet.

As if in slow motion, the rate of descent decreased, and they gradually began to go up again.

"Jesus," Christoph groaned. "We made it."

"I thought we were about to crash into the North Sea," Patrick's voice was trembling.

"Where are we?" Steinmann asked in a firm voice. "In the present? Your present?" He seemed remarkably unimpressed by the nosedive. He had probably been through more than his fair share of life-and-death situations.

"That's the million-dollar question," Christoph

answered. As the plane slowly climbed back up to a cruising altitude, he looked out of the window. "It was a dark night. Apart from the stars in the sky, he couldn't see a thing. He couldn't even make out the surface of the North Sea. He set the autopilot to an altitude of thirty thousand feet and a southerly course.

"I'm going to try the radio navigation. If we're back home, we should be able to make contact with the air traffic controllers."

He flipped a switch and checked the frequencies. Then he activated the microphone. He took a deep breath. "Bremen Center, XF39." There was a crackling in the speakers and then silence.

Christoph waited a moment and tried again. "Bremen Center, XF39."

Nothing.

His heart sank. "No response. On this frequency, there should be lots of radio traffic between air traffic controllers and planes flying over the North Sea."

He changed the frequency. "Bremen Center, XF39." Again, nothing. He tried another frequency. But even the ATIS of Hamburg Airport didn't respond. Then his eyes fell on the navigation display. The VOR he had tried to contact wasn't sending any signals either. And the GPS was silent. It could only mean one thing.

He needed a moment to gather himself. Then he turned to the others. The screens on Reuter's console cast a pale blue light across his face.

"I was mistaken," Christoph said flatly. "Everything here is dead. We're back in the devastated present of Steinmann's world. I'm sorry," he whispered.

"I told you so," Reuter said, without any triumph

in his voice.

"And now?" Patrick asked.

Christoph swallowed. They only had one option left. "We fly back through the wormhole to 1939 and land on the Thames. Let's hope we have enough fuel."

Christoph pressed the autopilot's course selector. The plane went straight into a curve.

"What about the fighter planes?" Steinmann asked.

"With a bit of luck they'll have gone back to their bases."

While Christoph turned the Airbus around onto a northerly course, nobody said a word. Two minutes later they were back on course for the wormhole.

"I'm going down to fifteen thousand feet," Christoph said hoarsely. He had no more energy left. It had been their last chance. It was all over. "Five minutes, then we're there. At least this time we can use the inertial navigation."

Suddenly, loud rock music blared through the cockpit. Christoph started. The music was coming from behind him, from the flight engineer's console. Christoph spun round. Reuter turned down the volume.

"What did you do?" Christoph asked.

"Turned on the radio," Reuter answered tersely, but he couldn't hide the surprise in his voice.

The music became quieter and a voice in an overly cheerful voice blared from the speaker. "That was the new hit from Coldplay, a great song!"

"Coldplay?" Steinmann asked.

"We'll be back in just a minute with more top hits!" the radio DJ continued. "But first, after the commercials, the six o'clock news!"

"Oh my God!" Patrick cried, eyes wide.

"What is Coldplay?" Steinmann wanted to know again.

"But that must mean ..." Reuter began.

"... that we're back home," Christoph ended his sentence. Why wasn't he receiving any radio signals or navigation? There were no errors displayed on the status screen. Maybe the onboard electronics had been affected when they were hit by the fighter planes? Christoph reset all the radio and navigation systems.

Meanwhile, they listened to the familiar commercials coming from the loudspeaker. Then the news began. "Good evening. It's six o'clock. No agreement has yet been reached in the tariff negotiations between the Deutsche Bahn and GDL. Politicians from both ruling parties called for an independent ..."

"We're definitely back home ..." Patrick said, and started to laugh.

New symbols appeared on the navigation display. The plane was receiving the signals of the VOR, and GPS coordinates appeared in front of Christoph's eyes. "We've got a connection!"

He picked up the microphone again. "Bremen Center, XF39?"

A few seconds silence, then an answer: "XF39, Bremen Center. We didn't expect to hear from you again."

Christoph joined in Patrick's laughter out of sheer relief. Even Reuter applauded.

"Bremen Center, XF39. We didn't either!"

He was given a course for Cologne and climbed to the stipulated altitude. Soon the lights of the towns and villages on the North Sea coast came into view.

"I never would have believed it!" Reuter said. "I was absolutely convinced we would come back out into Steinmann's world."

"Obviously we still have a lot to learn about the nature of time," Patrick said.

"I'm glad you were wrong, Reuter!" Christoph said.

Reuter laughed. "You know what? Me too!"

"Do we have enough fuel to get us to Cologne?" Patrick asked.

Christoph checked the screen and nodded. "Yes, just."

Steinmann had gotten out of his seat. He leaned over Christoph's shoulder and looked out of the window at the lights of Bremen glowing below. A lot of people were obviously still on their way home from work, because there was a long line of headlights snaking its way along Expressway 1.

"We're really in your present?"

Christoph grinned at him. "Yup, you bet!"

34

Christoph stood at the bottom of the steps. He watched as two uniformed military policeman led Werner away from the plane and shoved him into a green car with a blue light flashing on the roof.

"What will they do with him?" he asked Reuter, who was standing next to him.

He shrugged. "No idea. There won't be a public trial as long as the project is subject to secrecy. I need to discuss the case with my superiors in the ministries."

The flight back to Cologne had gone smoothly, although Christoph hadn't taken his eyes off the fuel gauge for a second. After he had finally parked the plane in front of the hangar and switched off the engines, there was only enough kerosene in the tanks to last another ten minutes.

He found out from a young project engineer that they had been gone two days. After they hadn't emerged from the wormhole as planned, they had been reported missing. The aircraft and its crew as well as the entire time travel project had already been written off by the big shots in Bonn and Berlin. Nobody had expected them to reappear, and apart from a few engineers who had desperately been trying to work out what had gone wrong, there was nobody in the hangar.

"Captain?"

"Yes?" Christoph turned around.

Franka, the young physicist, was standing in front of him with a big smile on her face. "I think we owe you a big thanks for getting us home safely."

Christoph shook his head. "No, we all—"

Without waiting for him to finish, she gave him a big hug and a soft kiss on the cheek. "Thank you!"

Then Frederik Schröder shook his hand. "I'm not the hugging type," he said with a smile.

One after another, the men and women who had accompanied him on this adventure stepped forward and gave him a hug, shook his hand, or patted him on the back. Christoph found it all a little embarrassing. It was enough for him to know they had all made it home in one piece.

Finally, Patrick stepped up to him. The engineer looked exhausted, as if he hadn't slept for weeks. "I'm driving home," he said in a tired voice. "See you soon."

"Thanks for your help in the cockpit."

Patrick nodded and disappeared without another word.

"That was close," Reuter said. "I just spoke with an intelligence officer. They tried to find the wormhole with an AWACS. But even with their upgraded infrared machines they couldn't find anything. It must have become unstable and collapsed shortly after our return." When Christoph didn't answer, he nodded in the direction of Steinmann, who was standing to the side, looking lost. "What do we do with him?"

The old man was watching in awed silence as one plane after another took off and landed. It was a busy evening at Cologne Airport.

"I'll take care of him," Christoph answered. He felt sorry for Steinmann. Although he no longer had to be afraid of dying of starvation or radiation, he was stranded in a strange world. It must all seem unbelievable to him. Christoph's house was big enough. He would let Steinmann live with him for a while and introduce him to this new world.

"That's very generous of you. It won't be easy," Reuter said.

Christoph nodded. "I know, he must feel like he's on Mars."

"I don't mean that," Reuter replied. "He's a nobody here. He has no identity. Strictly speaking, he isn't even a German citizen. He'll have to apply for asylum as a stateless person. I wonder how he'll explain his origins to the authorities."

Christoph shrugged. "I'll leave the bureaucracy to you."

"By the way," Reuter began quietly.

Christoph turned to look at him. What now?

"I misjudged you," Reuter said. "Before the flight, I mean. I was very impressed by your behavior. I revoke the termination of your contract. I would like you to stay."

"Stay?" Christoph asked in surprise. "To do what?"

Reuter pointed at the plane. Mechanics were going up the steps to the cabin, presumably to carry out the necessary maintenance on the plane and the time machine. "The last few days were tough, there's no denying that, but we learned a lot. And we will learn more!"

"What do you mean?"

"Our work has only just begun! We need to modify our project plan, but there are still so many unanswered questions about the nature of time. Imagine: we could explore all the different versions of history! We now know we can change the past to find out what would happen, but still return home to our world. Just think of everything we could learn!"

Christoph shook his head. He would never set foot in that plane again. "If I've learned anything from the last two days, it's that playing around with time is deadly. I kind of expected you to come to the same conclusion."

Reuter regarded him in silence.

"I quit!" Christoph said. "And if you want to do mankind a favor, destroy the time machine and all the blueprints."

Reuter was about to say something, but Christoph turned on his heel and left him standing there.

35

"How do you feel? Is everything OK?" Christoph asked Steinmann.

The old man tore his eyes away from a plane that had just come in to land, and looked at him. He had tears in his eyes, which glistened in the light of the landing lights. "How do I feel?" he whispered. "You cannot imagine how I feel. Look over there!" he pointed at the nearby cargo area of the airport, where workers in yellow safety vests were bustling about. "So many people. All these lights. The big planes. It's overwhelming." He hesitated. "It's as if I had traveled to another world."

"In a sense, that's exactly what you've done," Christoph answered quietly.

"How did you do it?" Steinmann asked. "I mean, how did you manage to stop the nuclear war? It seemed inevitable."

Christoph looked at the aircraft that had taken them to the past and another present. On the fuselage, just under the tail, were a row of bullet holes. A little higher and ... "We were lucky." He turned to look at Steinmann. "In the 1960s we came close to wiping ourselves out. But I guess our leaders learned from the horrors of the Second World War, and the images of Hiroshima and Nagasaki were fresh in their minds. They knew how the world would look if they pressed the red button." He put a hand on Steinmann's shoulder. "But that knowledge was gained at the price of millions of dead."

Was that really the reason? Or had they just been lucky? Christoph wanted to believe the victims of the Second World War hadn't died in vain. That the memory of the mass destruction of human lives guaranteed a safer future. But what would happen in a generation or two, when the knowledge of those horrors slowly faded from collective memory?

Christoph could see a technician standing in the cockpit of the aircraft checking the instruments. What had Reuter just said? The wormhole had disappeared shortly after they made it back. So what had happened to the world from which they had brought back Steinmann? Had it ceased to exist together with the wormhole? Or did it still exist outside of space and time? Maybe their present existed alongside an infinite number of other worlds. Maybe Elena was still alive in one of those worlds, living with another version of Christoph.

Probably he would never find out. But that made Christoph all the more aware of how important the present was. Yes, maybe it was possible to change the past, but it had no impact on the present. He needed to solve his problems in the here and now. Not in the past, and not in the future.

He took Steinmann by the arm and walked with him to the hangar.

"What are you thinking about?" Steinmann asked him.

Christoph took a deep breath. The November air was cool.

"About my son. And my grandson."

"Will you go and see them now?"

"No, I wouldn't be welcome."

"What happened?"

Christoph sighed. "I screwed up. My daughter-in-law, Andrea ... I never really liked her. I tried to talk him out of seeing her when they were still just friends."

"You didn't think she was good enough for your son?"

Christoph shrugged. "She was always quite aggressive. Not the kind of woman I would have chosen for my son."

"Isn't that natural?"

"I guess so, but then I really screwed up."

Steinmann didn't respond. Christoph had never spoken to anybody about it. Not even his wife. Only he, Michael, and Andrea knew about it. He wasn't sure why he felt the need to tell Steinmann about it.

"I told Michael I had seen Andrea with another man."

"Which wasn't true?" Steinmann asked.

"Exactly. But he didn't leave her. In fact, after he had talked it through with her, he married her. From that point on, our relationship was over."

"But I'm sure you apologized for your behavior?"

"I suppose so," he sighed. Of course, he had tried to at least respect Andrea once they were married. He had been almost overly friendly with her, trying to make her feel welcome in the family. But only now did he realize he had never actually apologized. He had always repressed or avoided it. How stupid, how vain! Their relationship would never improve until he asked her to forgive him for what he had done.

But what about Elena? Michael blamed him for her death, which up to now he had categorically denied. It was true that he hadn't caused the accident. But maybe Michael was right, all the same. He had always talked Elena into going on those weekend outings in the convertible, even though she wasn't particularly crazy about them. Yes, he could have admitted it, but he had been too proud for that, too.

"You should make up with your family," Steinmann said emphatically. "One day it might be too late.

Christoph nodded in silence. They had crossed the hangar and had reached the parking lot. Christoph beeped the car doors open. He helped Steinmann in and showed him how to buckle up. Then he got into the driver's seat.

"Shall I take you for a drive around the city center of Cologne?"

Steinmann considered for a moment and then shook his head. "No, not today. My head is already spinning from everything I've seen. I'd like to sleep ... Although I'm not sure I'll be able to."

"I'm sure you'll sleep well," Christoph reassured him.

"Where are you taking me?"

"You can come and live with me in Wiesbaden to start, until we find another solution. Since the death of my wife, I have plenty of room at home."

Steinmann nodded. "That's very kind of you. Thank you."

"In the next few days we'll look for somewhere for you to live. Reuter will make sure you get everything you need."

After a moment, Steinmann said: "I'm now in a world full of people, but I'll still be lonely. I don't know anybody."

"It's very easy to make friends," Christoph reassured him. He had an idea. Maybe there were people in this present whom Steinmann knew. But was it a good idea to look for them? It was worth a try. He just didn't know how to go about it. "Reuter wants to find out if there is a Herbert Steinmann in our present. Did you have any siblings?"

"No. You don't need to go to the trouble. Even if I were to find someone, they would be completely different people."

"What about your wife? Maybe some of her relatives are still alive. What was her maiden name?"

"Prandtl." Steinmann waved the idea aside. "But it's the same thing. She didn't have any relatives."

Christoph froze. "What did you say? What was your wife called?"

"Prandtl. Erika Prandtl. Why?"

Christoph couldn't breathe. Shaken, he searched Steinmann's features for a sign. Now he knew where he had seen this man before. Of course, Steinmann was much thinner than the man who had been slumped lifeless in his seat, but his face ...

"What is it?" Steinmann asked.

"Excuse me a moment. I need to make a short phone call."

"OK."

Christoph got out of the car and walked a little distance from the car before taking his cell phone out of his pocket. He needed to be sure!

He dialed her number. After half a minute, a soft female voice answered.

"Hello?"

"Wilder here."

"How can I help?"

"I have a question."

"Yes?"

"Your husband—"

"Yes?"

"His last name was Prandtl?"

"Yes, why?"

"That's your maiden name, isn't it?"

"Yes, that's correct. He took my name when we married."

So he was right!

"In the Third Reich his father was a high-ranking SS officer," Frau Prandtl explained. "He wanted to distance himself from his family by changing his name."

Christoph hesitated. What should he say? How should he say it?

"Mr. Wilder?"

Christoph took a deep breath. "I'm in the area. Could I drop by?"

"Do you know how late it is?"

"Yes, I know."

"Why do you need to see me?"

"It's about a favor you asked me."

"What was that?"

Christoph searched in vain for the right words.

"Well, OK, come by," Frau Prandtl said finally.

Christoph hung up. As he slowly returned to the car, he wondered if it was really such a good idea. He sat down, closed the door and started the engine.

"Is everything OK?" Steinmann asked, as Christoph maneuvered the car backward out of the parking space.

Christoph put the car into gear and drove off. "Yes, everything's fine. We're going to stop off at someone's house."

"Whose house?"

"Wait and see."

36

Christoph parked the car in front of the house.

"Come with me," he said, and helped Steinmann out of the car.

"Who lives here?"

Christoph didn't answer and led the man to the bottom of the steps. "Wait here a moment, please."

Steinmann nodded.

Christoph climbed up the steps, feeling a little queasy. He took a deep breath and rang the bell. A few seconds later, Mrs. Prandtl opened the door. Her eyes were glinting.

"Mr. Wilder. Please explain why you needed to see me at this late hour."

"You asked me to do something for you which I thought I could never do."

She looked at him blankly, then her eyes fell on Steinmann, who was standing at the bottom of the steps, cast in shadow. "Who is that?"

Christoph held out a hand to Steinmann and helped him climb the steps. His eyes fixed on the woman in disbelief. He stopped on the last step.

"Erika ...?" His lips were quivering.

Mrs. Prandtl froze. She grasped the door frame as if she didn't want to lose her balance. Although he was emaciated, she had clearly recognized him right away. She trembled.

"Herbert?" Her voice was hardly more than a whisper.

Steinmann approached her slowly and stopped just in front of his wife. "Erika? How is this possible?" He touched her arm with a trembling hand. She didn't draw away.

Christoph took a step back.

"Herbert!" she whispered again. "But how ...?" She ran her fingers tentatively over his face. They were gazing into each other's eyes.

They stood like that for a long time. Two people who had never met before and yet had shared their whole lives.

They looked at each other in silence and in wonder. Christoph could see disbelief, doubt, and hope in their eyes. Finally Mrs. Prandtl took him in her arms, sobbing. He buried his face in his wife's shoulder and wept bitterly.

Christoph turned away. He wasn't needed here. He went to his car, glanced back at the two people still standing in an embrace in the doorway.

He smiled as he got into the car. Maybe the whole horrific trip had been worth it for this alone.

Christoph started the engine and backed out onto the road. Time to go home and fall into bed, exhausted. Tomorrow was another day. He would go and see Michael and Andrea and ask for their forgiveness.

END

Did you like this book? Please rate this book on Amazon or write a small review on a book blog of your choice. Say what you liked about the book or what the author could improve in the future. Every review is a real help, especially for an indie author.

Thank you in advance.

You can also visit my blog if you'd like to find out anything new. There you can contact me directly:

http://www.petersonauthor.com

To find out the latest release dates, subscribe to the newsletter there.

Are you on Facebook? Visit the author's page at: http://www.facebook.com/PetersonAuthor.

You can also stay informed about new books on Twitter @Petersonauthor

Thank you

Phillip P. Peterson

Flight 39
April 2018

First published in German as:
Flug 39
July 2017

Author:
Phillip P. Peterson

Publisher:
Peter Bourauel
Josef-Dietzgen-Straße 3
D-53773 Hennef
contact@petersonauthor.com

German editors:
Anke Höhl-Keyser
Andrea Weil

Cover: 99designs

Translator:
Jenny Piening

English editor:
Laura Radosh

Phillip P. Peterson